"I can't!" he grated. "Forgive me. I should never...."

He'd left the bed. Was picking up his shirt, sweater...shoes he'd somehow discarded.

"You can't...go like this!" she gasped jerkily, raising herself on her elbows.

He stopped, his back to her. "I must!" he insisted.

"But...why? You wanted me!" she accused, deeply hurt, and unable to pacify her demanding body.

He remained silent, biting back an urge to tell her why he couldn't make love to her. Pounding relentlessly into his head had come the realization that he couldn't make love to the open and trusting Jodie under false pretenses. Either he had to tell her the whole truth of the situation or he had to leave her alone....

He's a man of cool sophistication.
He's got pride, power and wealth.
At the top of his corporate ladder, he's a
ruthless businessman, an *expert* lover—
His life runs like a well-oiled machine....

Until now. Because suddenly
he's responsible for a BABY!

HIS BABY
A miniseries from Harlequin Presents®.

He's sexy, he's successful...
and he's facing up to fatherhood!

There'll be another HIS BABY title out soon.

Sara Wood

MORGAN'S SECRET SON

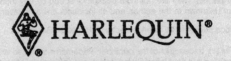

TORONTO • NEW YORK • LONDON
AMSTERDAM • PARIS • SYDNEY • HAMBURG
STOCKHOLM • ATHENS • TOKYO • MILAN • MADRID
PRAGUE • WARSAW • BUDAPEST • AUCKLAND

ISBN 0-373-12180-6

MORGAN'S SECRET SON

First North American Publication 2001.

Copyright © 2001 by Sara Wood.

This edition published by arrangement with Harlequin Books S.A.

Visit us at www.eHarlequin.com

Printed in U.S.A.

CHAPTER ONE

JODIE looked around the immaculate apartment, gave a satisfied twitch to her hip-hugging skirt and went to unbolt the door.

'Hi, Chas! Come in,' she invited amiably.

A flurry of New York's winter snow hurled itself past Chas's muffled figure and settled on the newly polished wood floor.

'You'll have to clear that up before it stains,' he directed, frowning at the innocent flakes. 'Hurry up! Fetch the—'

'No, Chas,' she purred, very cat-got-the-cream. 'I *won't*!'

She had no intention of slaving away for him. She was waiting for his reaction to her outfit, and when it came it was highly satisfying. Startled by her refusal, he looked her up and down and then did the tour again, all the way from her high-heeled red thigh boots to her new and classy hairstyle.

'Wowee, babe! You're a real knockout!' he declared in surprise.

She smiled to herself, thinking of the blow she was about to deal him. 'In more ways than one, Chas. Would you help me on with this?' she asked sweetly.

'Sure... Uh...are we going somewhere?'

He was more than puzzled by her assertive attitude, and his fingers hesitated on the warm amber-red jacket she'd handed to him.

'Just *me*!' she trilled.

Wonderfully in control, Jodie slipped her arms into the jacket then flung a heavy honey-gold cape around her shoulders, her once-nervy hands as steady as a rock. Then she dropped her bombshell.

'I'm leaving. Permanently. Here are my keys. The apartment's all yours. *You* go wipe the floor!'

He gaped. Jodie noticed for the first time that his teeth were rather uneven and his lips were thick and wet. She shuddered. Love really had been blind!

'But...but you're crazy about me!' he protested. 'And...I love you!'

'No,' she corrected, feeling contemptuous because he'd deliberately turned on his low, sexy voice. It was so gravelly it could have gritted Manhattan. But it did nothing for her. He was out of her system! She jammed her fabulous felt hat over her shiny chestnut bob and set the brim at a wicked angle. 'You love yourself and you love the person you tried to create,' she said, exulting in her coolness. 'Ever since I came into your office as a junior you've done your best to make me into what you wanted: a cross between a domestic servant, a hard-nosed career woman and an insatiable tigress in bed. I'm fed up with being on antidepressants because I don't measure up, and I'm sick of trying to work out some PR promotion for you whilst scrubbing saucepans in a *thong*!'

'You're exaggerating!' he gasped.

'Perhaps, but you can't deny that would have been your wildest dream come true!' Her eyes flashed, green and sparkling, as she warmed to her theme. 'No wonder I was a bag of nerves! No wonder this kitchen's seen more charred remains than a fire fighter on overtime! Well, if you want Superwoman, go train someone else. I want out.'

'You can't!' Chas said in desperation, as she picked up her new suede gloves purposefully.

'*Watch.*'

'But...we could have babies!'

She froze at his last-ditch, sneaky attempt to keep her, then swivelled around, her jade eyes glittering with such ferocity that Chas quailed. For the past six years she'd longed for marriage and children. Chas had refused.

'Good*bye*!' she said coldly. 'You can pick my car up from JFK airport!'

'You're not serious! Where's your luggage?' he scorned.

'In the car already.' Feeling free as a bird, she opened the door.

'Wait a minute! Where—where are you going?' he wailed.

'England,' she replied more softly, happiness lighting her face. 'To be with my father.'

'*Whaaat?* You're mad! I know he wrote to you, but that was six months ago and you haven't heard anything since! If he's the sort of guy to abandon you and your mother when you were barely a year old, he's hardly going to cheer when an emotional cripple lands on his doorstep!' Chas bellowed nastily.

'I'll ignore that vicious remark,' she said, utterly calm and collected. 'I fully understand why he might have changed his mind about seeing me. Anyone can get cold feet over a situation like this. But I've realised that I *have* to meet up with him. He's my only living relative and I have to *try*.'

Taking charge of her life was such fun! Why hadn't she done it long ago? Seven years she'd worked for Chas! For six of those she'd been living with him! She gave the stunned Chas an amused glance.

'You'll find the thongs and the push-up bras in my top drawer,' she murmured. 'Enjoy.'

Elated, she swept out into the snow. She felt gorgeous, dressed in new and sensual—rather than uncomfortable and tacky—underwear. Over it she wore an outrageously expensive tangerine silk T-shirt, the slim-fitting amber suit with its shockingly brief skirt, a theatrical cape, hat and boots. She had become a new woman in every way—and she was setting out on an adventure.

Seemingly all legs and slim suede boots, she wriggled into the driving seat, gave a little wave to the open-mouthed Chas and giggled. Then she drove away, her thoughts returning to that moment when she'd opened the letter for the first time.

The sincerity of her father's affection had burst upon her like a ray of sunshine and hope. *Your loving father, Sam,* he'd signed it, and the breath had caught in her throat when she'd read those words. Someone cared. Someone really loved and wanted her. The tears came to her eyes as she remembered and she had to hastily dash them away or end up flattened by a bus.

Her mother had died when she was small. Foster-parents had brought her up, and now she recognised that they had begun the curbing of her naturally happy, outgoing nature with their rigid rules and punishments. Love had never figured. Not true, unselfish, accepting love. But now things would be different.

Jodie beamed cheerfully at a cab driver who was trying to cut her up and she let him through with a friendly wave. She laughed out loud when the man hesitated, unable to believe what he was seeing. But she was on top of the world and in love with everyone—Chas excepted!—even cab drivers.

Soon, she thought dreamily, she'd be arriving at her father's house in the south of England. He would have her letter announcing her arrival by now, and he could hardly refuse to see her when she'd come so far.

Just in case he did, there was Plan B. She'd booked into

a nearby hotel, from where she planned to work on his heartstrings until he agreed to a meeting.

She felt sure he wouldn't reject her. Something, someone, had dissuaded him from answering her many letters, she was sure. She understood only too well how other people could cloud one's judgement.

It had taken her this long to realise that Chas's advice—to forget her father—had been totally selfish. For years she'd relied on Chas, becoming increasingly dependent and subservient. But now she saw him for what he was: a bully and a control freak.

Her present confidence came from the fact that her father had been so eager for her to visit, and had even asked for her mother's address. A pang went through her. The weeks of loneliness and bewilderment after her mother's death had been so awful that she could recall them with crystal-clearness even now.

That was all over, though. Her eyes sparkled. This was the happiest she'd ever been in the whole of her life. No clouds on the horizon, no thongs, and a case stuffed to the brim with sizzling citrus and scarlet clothes!

'Brace yourself, England,' she cried with a laugh, seeing the sign for the airport. 'Here I come!'

With Jack hooked expertly over his shoulder and his hands slippery with suds, Morgan finally succeeded in opening the door.

Why did people always call when he'd just got the baby in the bath? It was one of life's irritating mysteries—and it was getting beyond a joke.

He grunted when the postman's cheery, gossip-ready face hove into view. Village life in rural Sussex had its drawbacks. People expected to chat, to share information.

And there were too many busybodies around trying to find out what the devil he was doing in Sam Frazer's house.

The postman had taken a step back. Morgan realised he'd been scowling and modified the severity of his expression.

'Morning,' he muttered. It still sounded like a veiled threat, even to his ears. Must do better!

'Recorded delivery,' the postman said, warily handing over the package.

'Thanks,' he said, mustering a little more grace.

He signed for the letter with his free hand and gave it a cursory glance. For Sam. He dropped it onto the pile of unopened mail on the hall table which was waiting till Sam's health improved, and made to shut the door. He had a million things to do.

'Er…baby all right?' enquired the postman meekly.

With a concealed sigh, Morgan mused that curiosity must be stronger than fear.

'Fine.'

'Must be five weeks old now. I love kids. Can I have a peep?'

It would have been churlish in the extreme to refuse, tempting though it was. Resigned to having Jack poked about by any number of strangers in the next few months, he pushed back the folds of the hooded towel which he'd wrapped around Jack's wet body and his face softened as two tiny boot-black eyes stared back at him.

'Like his father,' observed the postman, making funny faces for Jack's benefit.

'Is he?'

How a snub-nosed scrap of humanity could look anything like an adult, he couldn't imagine! Ironically everyone declared that Jack resembled Sam.

Guilt and resentment sucked relentlessly at his stomach. It was terrible being torn in two like this… He stared bleakly at the baby, despising himself for what he'd done, almost sick with anger and worry.

'We were all sorry to hear Mr Frazer had been rushed into hospital again. How *is* he?' persisted the postman with genuine sympathy.

'Critical,' Morgan jerked, all hell breaking loose in his heart.

'That's bad! He's had some rotten luck since he moved in last summer.' The postman patted his hand comfortingly. 'It was a nice funeral you gave his missus,' he said soothingly. 'Lovely oration.'

Morgan winced and didn't correct him. Teresa hadn't been married to Sam—a fact which had virtually caused her death.

He supposed that the postman was trying to be kind, but Morgan did not want to be reminded too vividly of that terrible day when he'd stood in the driving rain watching Teresa's coffin being lowered into the ground.

And then there'd been the expressions of sympathy to deal with. Teresa's London friends knew his secret: that he'd had an affair with her, before she'd switched to Sam.

They had stared with open curiosity at his hollow eyes and shocked appearance, whispering salaciously behind their hands.

He had known what they were saying. He'd overheard a comment: 'Did he never stop loving her? Is that why he's so distraught?'

The knife twisted even more sharply in his guts. What a hypocrite he was, a sham, a fraud! God! reliving it all was unbearable. He had to get away.

'Thanks,' he croaked, and had to stop to clear his throat of the clogging emotion.

The postman took advantage. 'Good on you for looking

after their baby—not many men would do that. Close relative, are you?'

'Not exactly. Excuse me,' he said stiffly, before the relationship could be investigated—and endlessly dissected during some idle coffee morning. 'His bath water's getting cold.'

He shut the door with a sigh of relief and instinctively hugged Jack closer, as if that could protect him from anything bad anyone might say or do.

But danger had literally threatened. Perhaps it was just as well that Sam had been rejected by his daughter. She would have jeopardised Jack's future. And that, Morgan thought darkly, was something he couldn't bear.

The baby felt soft and warm against his chest and a lump came back into Morgan's throat as emotion spilled in a flood of liquid heat through his body.

Teresa's death had stunned him. It had been the last thing he'd expected. And now…

What had he got himself into? The deception was getting harder to maintain. Every time he visited Sam the secret of Jack's birth burned inside him like a red-hot poker, souring his relationship with the man he admired and respected and loved more than any other.

Morgan groaned. Blurting out the truth would make him feel a hell of a lot better—but it would crucify Sam. Probably catapult him into a fatal decline.

'I can't do it!' he rasped in despair.

But…he loathed deceit and despised people who were so feeble they had to tell lies.

His eyes darkened with pain as he tried to face the inevitable and make the ultimate sacrifice. The truth would have to be locked up inside him and never revealed while Sam lived, however much that went against his own wishes and desires. There were two people weaker than himself involved, and they had needs greater than his.

'Jack... How small and defenceless you are... And yet you don't know the trouble you've caused, little one,' he said quietly to the baby, who gave him that black glass stare and rooted around with his mouth, blind instinct prompting him to search for his non-existent mother's breast.

'Poor little scrap,' Morgan whispered, offering a knuckle in compensation. The small mouth clamped around it, digging in hard, and the black lashes fluttered in bliss. 'No wonder Sam adores you,' Morgan murmured, enchanted as always. 'You'd make anyone's heart soften. Let's get to that bath and make you all clean for your...'

He couldn't say it. Some things were impossible to deal with, and assigning fatherhood was one insurmountable hurdle he hadn't yet come to terms with.

Morgan took the baby up to the nursery feeling like a heel. He was caught in a web of lies. Here he was, fooling Jack with a knuckle to suck instead of the real thing. And in the future he'd be deceiving the child every single day of his life.

But he didn't want to! Stricken, he stopped in mid-stride, fighting the souring anger, desperately trying to suppress his own needs. All his paternal instincts—previously hidden even to himself—were clamouring for the truth to be known. His head told him that was impossible. Head versus heart. A soul-destroying battle. Which would prevail?

Anguish distorted his features. Emotion flooded unchecked within him, his customary tight self-control eroded by exhaustion and shock.

For a terrifying moment he felt an overwhelming need to throw back his head and let rip a primal yell of anger and frustration. Only the presence of the child stopped him.

Slowly his heart rate became regular again as the anger became ruthlessly suppressed.

For Jack's sake he gritted his teeth and continued the interrupted bath rituals, blocking out everything but the immediate needs of the tiny, dependent baby.

When he'd finished they settled in front of the log fire in the drawing room, and as Jack sucked enthusiastically on the bottle Morgan watched, his harrowed features relaxing into a deep awe. This was his compensation, the joy amid the grieving.

To him, the child was a miracle of perfection. Dark-haired, flawless skin, thick black lashes. Smiling, he touched the little hand with its long, slender fingers and minute fingernails. Jack's hand curled around his finger in an impressive grip of possession. Morgan's heart ached.

This was his son, and he wanted everyone to know it.

CHAPTER TWO

BLEAKLY he acknowledged the impossibility of that dream. 'Sam will be proud of you,' he promised with an effort.

The urgent hungry expression on Jack's face was slowly vanishing and a soft, blissful look of repose had begun to replace it. The small features smoothed out, the impossibly arched mouth slackened with sleep.

Desperate for sleep himself, Morgan adjusted his arm so that the two of them could rest in comfort. Just a few minutes for a catnap, he promised himself vaguely. Unfortunately his teeming thoughts wouldn't allow him to rest.

He hadn't found a daily help yet, and the kitchen needed clearing up. After that, he had to sterilise a load of bottles, make up a new batch of feed, put the washing on and do some ironing. Some time today he had to ring the office to see if it still existed. Then he and Jack would wrap up and go to see Sam.

He groaned at the catalogue of things which needed doing. It was eleven-thirty and he hadn't even shaved—let alone found time to grab a morning coffee! But when he wasn't by Sam's bed, doing essential chores or looking after the baby, he was pacing the floor night after night, and his energy levels were at rock bottom.

More to the point, his mind was consumed with guilt. He'd never done anything wrong in his life before and this secret was testing his self-respect and control to the limit.

He knew he was on a short fuse. Was it any wonder? Morgan's black brows screwed together in a fierce frown.

His big capable hands curled around the tiny baby who slept, oblivious to everything around him. Jack made Morgan feel both protective and envious.

His eyes grew hazy as he contemplated the future. For years he'd done whatever he'd wanted, gone where he'd pleased, lived as free as a bird. Now circumstances had clipped his wings and it was hard to adjust.

Once he had been free to fly to exotic sites and absorb their meaning, to discover that feverish excitement of seeing one of his designs take shape on his drawing board—and then grow in reality on the site, at one with its environment.

But in one brief moment with Teresa Frazer he had created and designed something which had turned his world upside down. For the rest of his life he'd never forget the moment when he'd turned up at the hospital and she had confessed that Jack was his son, not Sam's. Jack had been conceived while they were still together—before Sam even knew of Teresa's existence.

He winced, seeing again that once-beautiful face, hideously mangled by the car crash which had brought him hurrying to Sussex from his London flat. He hadn't doubted her word for a second. She had been so desperate to tell the truth, and too aware that she was close to death to waste her time with lies.

Morgan thought of Sam's breakdown when news of the crash had come through, how it had been he, Morgan, who'd been with Teresa for her last conscious moments before the emergency Caesarean.

It had been *he* who'd first held his baby, *he* who'd wept with unrestrained joy and amazement. He hadn't shed tears since he was eleven, but the suddenness of fatherhood had overwhelmed him.

Emotion had filled his heart to bursting. He'd wanted this

child. *His* child! And yet he had known even then that he'd have to surrender him for the sake of a slowly dying man. Jack must be registered as Sam's son.

Such joy and sorrow mingling together as he had never known...

Morgan passed a shaky hand over his face. He owed *everything* to Sam. But this was the cruellest price to pay!

Racked with despair, he bent his weary head and gently kissed the downy forehead. The warmth of the fire and the accumulation of several sleepless nights began to blur his mind. His thoughts became less focused and finally he slept, briefly free from his troubles and the destructive, shameful deceit.

The closer Jodie came to the village where her father lived, the more breathless and excited she became. Discovering his existence had been the most wonderful thing that had happened to her. Her heartbeat quickened. She dearly wanted this to work. It *must*! All her hopes were resting on it.

Her eager eyes took in the scenery with its voluptuously smooth hills—incongruously called Downs, according to the map. Sheep grazed on the emerald grass of the tiny fields and swans were lazily decorating a meandering river.

And then she saw it: an old-fashioned signpost pointing the way down a country lane. She turned off the main road, her heart singing with unrestrained delight.

It was getting dark, even though it was only about four o'clock in the afternoon. In her headlights she could pick out quaint flintstone cottages strung out sporadically along the lane. Occasionally there would be a small Tudor cottage, with black and white timbers, a thatched roof and pretty garden.

As she passed each house she slowed the car to a crawl,

so she could read the names, her mouth increasingly dry with nerves. At last, in the rapidly fading light, she spotted the one she was looking for: Great Luscombe Hall.

'Be there!' she begged in a heartfelt plea.

Nervously she headed down a long drive, her hands gripping the steering wheel in a mixture of panic and anticipation. Her forest dark eyes widened. There was a moat! Awed, she steered the car over the wooden bridge that spanned it. It had never occurred to her for a minute that her father might be wealthy!

Adjusting to this fact, Jodie brought the car to a halt in front of the house. Her heart was beating hard in her chest with anticipation. Great Luscombe Hall was a rambling, timbered manor house with a roof made from huge slabs of stone, and its façade had been constructed with enough oak beams to make a fleet of ships.

'I can't believe this!' she whispered.

With trembling fingers she switched off the lights and the engine and leapt out, her body tensed in expectancy.

And then she heard a furious barking. She shrank back, terrified to see a Collie hurtling towards her.

'Help!' she croaked, freezing to the spot. Her terror-stricken gaze was pinned to the dog's white fangs. 'G-g-good, dog!' she squeaked unconvincingly.

'He's friendly,' snapped a hard male voice. 'His tail's wagging, can't you see?'

Her father! Forgetting the animal, she looked hopefully towards the house, a warm, happy smile bursting forth and illuminating her eyes. It faded almost immediately. This couldn't be him. He was too young. This was...who?

She swallowed nervously. The dishevelled, raven-haired man was glaring at her suspiciously from the shadowy doorway. Darkness surrounded him, a mere chink of light coming from the door he'd pulled to, as if he were defending his castle from intruders.

Extreme tiredness made her head swim with odd, fanciful images—the black-watered moat, the medieval manor and with its looming, jettied upper storey, and the sinister stranger.

She noted that his hair was wild and wind-tousled, his black brows thick and fierce and the angular jaw covered in five o'clock shadow. Wide-eyed with apprehension, she took in his hostile stare, crumpled crew-neck sweater and jeans and wondered if she'd come to the wrong house.

'Great...Luscombe Hall?' she queried shakily.

'Yes!' he clipped.

No mistake, then. And he was just a man, she reminded herself. Bad-tempered, unfriendly and unwittingly threatening, but nothing more. It was time her adrenaline climbed down to normal.

'Then, hi!' she called, rallying her spirits. When she took a step forward she felt the dog's nose against her thigh and her courage faltered. 'You're *sure* I can move without losing a leg or two?' she asked, worried.

Searingly dark eyes brooded on her poppy-coated lips and she felt the hairs rise on the back of her neck. He'd just stared, that was all. But a flash of something almost sexual had slid briefly through her body.

'He's eaten already,' he dismissed. His mouth remained hard, as if hacked from granite by a sculptor who didn't know how to do curves. 'You want something?' he shot.

It wasn't the most gracious welcome she'd ever had! Jodie thought he sounded as if he'd got out of the wrong side of bed—and not long ago, judging by his rumpled state. Who could he be—the gardener? No—he'd been indoors. And the house might look grand enough for a butler, but not one who looked so untidy and...dangerous.

Handyman perhaps. He could have been under the floor-boards fixing something, hence his mussed-up hair.

Mystified, Jodie risked walking to the house. The dog bounded about her, circling as if she were a wayward sheep to be brought into line, and she smiled at its antics—though her city upbringing stopped her from trusting it enough to offer it a friendly pat.

'Here, Satan!' ordered the man sharply.

She hid a grin. Satan! That said volumes about his owner! She watched thoughtfully as the dog whirled around and flew over to its master, sitting to heel and gazing up anxiously. How severely had the dog been chastised till that level of obedience had been achieved? Fresh from living with a bully of her own, she felt her dislike of the man rack up a notch.

Close up, he seemed to tower over her slender frame, and she felt almost smothered by the tense atmosphere which surrounded him. It was clear from his manner that he was harassed and impatient, suggesting he had better things to do. Boilers to repair, pipes to lag, she thought with a sublime ignorance about maintenance. So she got to the point.

'I've come to see my father,' she told him briskly, though her joy suddenly shone through as she thought of their imminent meeting. Her fears vanished completely and she beamed, suddenly awash with happiness. This was a moment to cherish.

The man drew in his breath sharply and his eyebrows collided fiercely over his nose, as if she'd just confirmed his worst suspicions.

'Your...*father*?' he repeated ominously.

'Sam Frazer,' she confirmed, before the frown screwed up the man's entire face.

'*Sam!*'

He looked devastated. He'd gone quite pale beneath his olive complexion. Jodie took pity on him. Thinking only that she was seconds away from seeing her father for the first time, she gave an ecstatic grin and said, 'Yes! It's going to surprise a lot of people, I imagine. I'm pretty knocked out too—this house isn't what I'd expected at all. I'd imagined my father in a little cottage with roses over the door, and wearing tweedy things with leather patches on the elbows. This is really grand!'

'Is it?'

Jodie's voice faltered a little at the contempt in the man's eyes. But she wasn't to be put off. 'Sure it is. Now, if you're wondering, I'm his long-lost daughter from New York,' she explained. 'You'll want credentials, I suppose. Understandable. You can't let anyone in, can you? Somewhere...I have his letter...' Eagerly she scrabbled in her bag and produced it. 'It's a bit blurred in places because I cried over it,' she pointed out hurriedly. 'And it's coming apart at the folds because—'

'I get the picture,' he said tightly.

He shot her an unreadable look from under his brows then switched on the porch light and bent his tousled head to study the first few lines. Jodie restrained her urge to leap about from one foot to the other and yell, Let me in—now! and contented herself with idly observing him as an exercise in self-discipline.

It surprised her to see that his hair was gorgeous: thick and silky, gleaming with the brilliance of a raven's wing in the light. Her thick brown lashes fluttered with unwilling feminine admiration as her gaze took in his killer looks and the sheer masculinity of his angled jaw and powerful shoulders. Then her eyes widened in wonder. There were some creamy stains on his black sweater.

She was just pondering on this odd fact when the hairs

began to rise on the back of her neck and she sensed that he must be studying her again, with that bone-slicing stare. She looked up and gasped. His expression was one of utter repugnance.

'He wrote this six months ago,' he said icily.

'I *know* that! I replied immediately—'

'Really?'

'Yes!' Her face went hot at his disbelief. 'I did!' Her brow furrowed when she realised what his doubt must mean. 'Are you telling me that my father didn't get my letters?' she asked in dismay.

'Correct.'

Exasperated by the monosyllabic responses, she drew her brows into an even deeper frown.

'That's impossible. I wrote several times in quick succession—and I telephoned twice—' she said with dignity.

'If that were true—*if*,' he interrupted coldly, 'why did you come?'

Her eyes widened. 'Because I want to see him, of course! Something doesn't add up here. I sent those letters. They can't all have been lost.'

'I agree. He had no letters from you. So you must be lying. I think you'd better leave.'

She glared and clenched her fists in angry distress, her mouth beginning to tremble. Hot tears pricked the backs of her eyes. It would be tragic if this was as far as she got! So near, so far...

'I'm not going till I see my father! I *did* write!' she insisted in desperation. 'Something's happened to the mail. A wrong zip code, maybe. I spoke to a woman on the phone. I'm not imagining that. I asked for Sam Frazer, said who I was, and she told me he didn't want to see me—'

'Well, that final comment is true, at least,' he drawled. 'I suggest you turn around and go home.'

He'd turned and was about to shut the door when she lunged forward and jammed herself in the gap. The dog barked excitedly, its teeth snapping close to her thigh.

'Ouch!' she gasped. 'Get this door and this dog off me!'

The pressure of the door was removed from her protesting flesh.

'Leave!' ordered the man.

Glowering, she stayed put; the dog backed away obediently. She rubbed her arm and thigh, conscious that she was deliberately being intimidated by the man's looming bulk.

'What did you do that for?' he asked impatiently. And then, with a small thread of concern in his voice, 'Are you hurt?'

'It's nothing,' she dismissed. 'But I couldn't let you slam the door in my face. I've flown across the Atlantic to see my father. Surely he can spare a few moments of his time?'

'No. He can't.'

Her imploring face lifted to his. 'Just a few moments... I won't bother him for long, but... You must let me in,' she said, her voice trembling with emotion. '*Please!* You've no idea what it's like not to know your father! I need to see him so badly—even if it's just the *once* and never again! It's not much to ask, surely? To see what he looks like, to hear his voice...' Her own voice cracked up annoyingly. 'I—I don't even have a *photograph*! Let me have memories of him to take away with me, if nothing else,' she added in a croaky husk. 'Imagine how you'd feel in my position!'

'Hell.' His growl was followed by a long pause, as if he was struggling against his better judgement. Jodie waited with bated breath, willing him to relent. 'You'd better come in,' he muttered grudgingly, to her great relief.

Then, before she could gather her wits, he'd turned on

his heel and was walking into the beamed hall beyond, the dog at his side. She stared at his daunting back with irritation. This guy wasn't a servant to anyone. He oozed authority with every flicker of his ink-dark eyes. He wasn't pleasant, either.

But everything pointed to the fact that he knew her father well. And the hostile welcome must be because he knew that her father had been disappointed and upset when her expected letters didn't arrive.

No. Correction. There was another reason. This guy *might* be the person who'd dissuaded her father from going ahead with the reunion. If so, she had to persuade the guy that he had nothing to fear from her.

Jodie gave a feeble smile. Fear! He wouldn't be afraid of the devil himself if he came calling!

Suddenly she started, remembering the recorded delivery. That must have arrived—proof enough! She would call his bluff.

In seconds she crossed the dark oak floor and caught hold of the man's arm. It felt hard and muscled as it tensed beneath her fingers. His whole body became stiff and taut, as if she'd invaded his space. Crushed by his cold dislike, she let her hand slide away.

'I'm sorry,' she said hastily. 'But I had to stop you before you reported back to my father. I want you to know I'm not lying. I can prove that I had the right address and that he must have had my letters.'

The hard, uncompromising gaze pierced into her brain and she felt giddy.

'How?'

With an effort, Jodie pulled herself together. She might be tired and woozy, but this was important.

'I sent a letter by recorded delivery to say I was coming. It must have been safely delivered into the right hands; it's guaranteed! And if that arrived, then so did all the other letters!' she said in triumph.

'Ah.'

She followed his gaze to a circular table which groaned under a pile of unopened mail. Her letter lay on the top. Her mouth opened in amazement that anyone could be so cavalier.

'How can you claim the rest of my mail's gone astray?' she exclaimed in horror. 'It's probably all lurking beneath that heap!'

'No. That's just ten days' worth,' he said curtly.

'Ten...! But you can't leave mail unopened! And where are my previous letters, then? In a landfill site?' she spluttered, aghast.

'Don't be ridiculous! All his earlier mail has been dealt with. So will this when... You look hot,' he said, changing the subject abruptly. 'Let me take your cape.'

He came up behind her and his hands were on her shoulders before she could move. But his touch seemed tentative, as if he would have preferred to avoid contact. The pure wool cape slid away, slithering across her firm breasts in a shimmer of gold.

'Your hat,' he ordered, appearing in front of her and holding out his hand.

He looked her up and down, and then again—perhaps startled by the vibrancy of her colour scheme, she thought with a flash of amusement. She let a smile sneak out, her hopes rising—she'd got this far at least. What did she care what had gone wrong in the past? This was now and she was here, and somewhere in this house was her own dear father.

Jodie removed her hat with a flourish, giving her head a little shake as she did so.

'Let's not get twitchy over what happened. There's obviously been a muddle. The important thing is that I see him now,' she said happily, silky brown hair still swinging around her delighted face.

His lips tightened into an uncompromisingly grim line. 'Come into the study,' he ordered.

She was left with her mouth open in astonishment as he strode away. This, she decided angrily, was another control freak. He told women to jump; they asked How high? Chauvinist!

She followed, the dog prowling alongside her, but she paused on the threshold of the lamp-lit room he'd entered. Her father wasn't there. Her hands curled into angry fists as she checked the room again.

The stranger stood with his feet planted firmly apart in an attitude of domination. He leant, squire-like, against a carved beam which spanned an enormous recess...an inglenook, she decided, raking around in her mind for her limited knowledge of medieval houses.

Logs the size of small tree trunks crackled and blazed in a massive iron basket, filling the timbered room with the sweet aroma of pine. Books lined the walls and a desk, chaotically littered with papers, sat squarely in a mullioned bay window, its deep window seat backed by a dozen or so scarlet cyclamen in oriental pots.

'You're busy, I'm in a hurry, so I won't hold you up any longer,' she said, her chin high. 'You know why I'm here. Tell me where my father is!'

Her face went hot. He was examining her in intense detail and warmth was creeping through her as he did so.

'Sit!' he ordered.

'Good grief! What do you think I am—a dog?' she declared indignantly.

'I was talking to Satan. He's just behind you in the doorway. Perhaps you'd like to sit down as well, though?' he suggested, a faintly dry humour briefly appearing in his eyes.

She grinned. At last he was beginning to unbend a little. 'Sorry!' she said blithely. 'I'm not used to orders being barked at dogs.'

His eyebrow rose at her implied criticism. 'Collies are intelligent and powerful. He knows he's not allowed in the reception rooms, though he tries it on every now and then. You rule them, or they rule you. All dogs need a pack leader.'

'And you're it?' she said with a smile, wondering if his philosophy extended to women.

'For the moment. Please, make yourself comfortable.'

The cream leather armchair he'd indicated looked as welcoming as a warm bed and she sank into it in relief. 'That's better! It's been a long journey,' she confided, stretching her long limbs luxuriously and giving a little wriggle to ease her stiffness. 'I've been driving on the left side of the road for the past four hours and my brain has been protesting every inch of the way. I suppose I could have stopped overnight somewhere, but I kept going because I longed to be here.'

Misty-eyed again, she ventured a smile, but received nothing in return.

'I'll get you some tea,' he drawled. 'Stay!' he ordered.

Jodie wasn't too sure if this had been directed to her or the dog. 'I'd rather see my father straight away,' she said hurriedly. But not quickly enough. His long jean-clad legs had swallowed up space so quickly that he was almost out of the room. Balked again, she called, 'And if it's no trouble, I'd prefer coffee... Oh, for heaven's sake!' she fumed in exasperation.

Morgan strode to the kitchen, and once he was there and

out of sight he stopped dead, knowing he had to gather his composure before he faced Jodie again.

He needed space. Time. A brain that wasn't fuzzy with exhaustion and which could deal with the problem her arrival had created.

Focus. He must concentrate... Cursing softly to himself, he ruthlessly shut out everything but the alarming situation.

He had a choice. To refuse Jodie any access to Sam, or—when Sam's health improved—he could coax Sam to see his daughter. He closed his eyes, fighting for objectivity.

If he could persuade her to go then life could continue as before. And one day Jack would return to him.

He felt dark emotions swirling inexorably in his mind, denying him clarity of thought. Because he knew with a gut-wrenching pain that if Jodie was ever reunited with Sam then he could lose his son for ever.

Jodie was Sam's next of kin. When Sam died, which the doctors said would be within a year or two, she would automatically be responsible for Jack's future welfare.

And he, Morgan, would be out on his ear.

A devil was driving him, whispering in his ear wickedly that he could eliminate all danger by stating the cold, unvarnished truth: that her father had rejected her utterly. It would be so simple—and he wanted his son so badly that he tortured himself by listening to the voice in his head even though he knew he should, in all honour, endeavour to bring father and daughter together.

But Sam had been adamant. 'She's like her mother!' he'd declared with wild conjecture, when he'd given up all hope of hearing from Jodie. 'Selfish, flighty and heartless! If she knew I was rich she'd be here quick enough! Morgan, she's broken my heart! I never want to see her—even if she turns up in rags and trailing ten children in her wake, *do you hear*?' he'd raged.

'I hear,' he'd said quietly, hoping some day to dissuade him.

But that had been before Morgan knew he was Jack's father. And now Jodie was here, in dazzling scarlet and trailing fire and passion and a steely determination in her wake.

Common sense told him that he should send her away with a photo after a cup of tea. But could he live with himself, knowing that Sam had had the opportunity to enjoy the last year or two of his life in his daughter's loving company?

'God!' he muttered. 'What a choice!'

Hard on himself, as always, he forced himself to go through the motions of making tea, but his fingers were constantly stilled by the strangely haunting image of Jodie's face.

What was it about her? Some element of Sam, his honesty, his goodness? It would have been easier if she'd been an out-and-out cow—selfish, flighty and heartless, as Sam had suggested.

But Morgan's lasting image of her was of her transparent, innocent joy, which had cut through his suspicion and shock like a sword of light.

He stared into space, seeing the blinding smile which had lit up her extraordinary jade eyes till they'd sparkled like gemstones. She'd seemed almost vulnerable in her eagerness to tell him about herself.

Morgan thought of her passion when she'd begged for a crumb, the right to see what her father looked like because she had no photographs of him. Her words had sliced through his heart like a knife through butter. He understood that terrible emptiness of being somehow unfinished because of an unknown parent.

All his life he'd wanted to know who *his* father was. His rootlessness, his avoidance of committal and his dangerous hunger for love had undoubtedly been a consequence of that empty gap in his life. In that instant he had felt a visceral stab of compassion for her. And so he'd weakened.

Of course she was lying about the letters. But it was like the lie of a vulnerable child who can't bear to be in the wrong. A greedy child, perhaps, he reminded himself with a frown, before he became too indulgent. Maybe she'd done some research on the Internet and had discovered that Sam Frazer was one of the most prestigious architects in the country.

He rubbed a thoughtful hand over his stubble. With Sam owning half the village and the lucrative practice, she'd be in line for a huge inheritance. And custody of Jack.

Morgan's hands shook as he filled the kettle. Where would that leave him? Visiting occasionally. Looking on while she brought up his son.

'No!' he muttered vehemently. 'Never in a million years!'

Sam only had a short time to live. Morgan had planned to adopt Jack when the older man died. But if Jodie was on the scene she would be firmly entrenched as Jack's carer by then.

There'd be a legal tussle which could go on for years, with Jack in the middle—and by that time Jodie would to all intents and purposes be a mother figure to Jack. He couldn't take his son away under those circumstances. It would be too cruel.

No! Better if he never let that situation arise. He sucked in a harsh breath. That settled it. He'd keep her at arm's length and respect Sam's explicit wishes. Tea and sympathy, then pack her off home.

CHAPTER THREE

JODIE sat fuming and twiddling her fingers. She flicked through an elaborately illustrated book about buildings in Brazil, which normally would have interested her, but she had one thing only dominating her mind: her father.

She knew she was ready to fall asleep from sheer exhaustion—but before she did she must see him. Over tea—*coffee!*—which would revive her and give her the boost her system needed, she'd ask this man if...

No, she'd demand. She was no collie dog. She would not be ruled by him.

Wearily she hauled herself from the chair and followed the sounds of movement, finding herself in the doorway of an enormous farmhouse kitchen fitted out with limed wood units in the country house style.

Unobserved and unheard in her rubber soles, she temporarily forgot why she'd come because he was wearily dumping leaf tea into a pot like a zombie on sedatives. Intrigued, Jodie counted six spoonfuls before he paused and then uttered a brief expletive.

Each one of his movements was slow and laboured as he emptied the pot and then carefully recounted the correct amount of tea in a voice which betrayed his irritation with himself.

After adding boiling water to the brew, a deep sigh welled up from the depths of his body. His head tipped back in an attitude of despair.

Jodie was fascinated. He seemed more than tired. It was

as if life itself had become untenable. Why? What was going on here?

Not daring to let him know she'd seen him in an unguarded moment, she tiptoed away and made the approach again, ensuring that she made enough noise on her way to the kitchen to serve as a warning.

When she entered, he was back in control of himself again: stiff, erect, and poker-faced.

'I thought I'd see if I could help,' she began crisply. 'And—'

'It's done,' he said, before she could ask for a coffee. 'Now that you're here, we might as well have tea in here instead. Milk or lemon?'

'Whatever.' Jodie was too eaten up with curiosity to pursue her preference and she sat down at the scrubbed pine table expectantly. Tea was a stimulant, anyway. And she needed revitalising before she started making waves. 'Now,' she continued amiably, hoping to disarm him, 'tell me who you are.'

'Morgan Peralta.'

'Unusual name,' she said, encouraging him to open up.

'I have Colombian parents,' he replied grudgingly.

It explained a good deal: his dark good looks, the sense of lurking volcanic passions, the Latin cheekbones and bred-in-the-bone sensuality. He had a magnificent body: just muscled and lean enough for her taste. Beside him, Chas would look a slob. So would most men.

She looked at his hands, always a give-away, and thought that there was something very sensual in the way his slender—almost graceful—fingers dealt with slicing the lemon. He'd be good with women, she mused. Delicate in his touch. Tantalisingly exploring... She blinked, startled by where her thoughts had taken her.

Feeling warm from the heat of the kitchen, Jodie unbuttoned her jacket. She would have removed it but Morgan's hooded gaze had honed in like a guided missile on the tangerine shirt beneath and she felt a sudden frisson of sexual danger as something indefinable sizzled briefly between them.

Stupid. How could he possibly be interested in her? It was her over-developed imagination. Static in the air. Besides, he was hardly going to jump her. Not over tea!

She hid a smile at her caution but decided she'd feel more comfortable if she kept the jacket on. The T-shirt fitted snugly and she didn't want Morgan counting her ribs. Or anything else...

She was astonished to feel a blush creep up her entire body, and she let out a breath she hadn't known she was holding.

Morgan slanted an odd look at her from under his brows then sat opposite her, immediately picking up the teapot and pouring out a thin, almost gold-coloured liquid into their cups and slipping in a slice of lemon. Jodie accepted the offered cup doubtfully. It didn't look like any tea she'd ever seen.

'I'm Jodie,' she offered, anxious to be accepted. 'Jodie Frazer.'

'I know.'

He was close to her father, then. She took a deep breath and plunged in.

'I imagine my father was upset when he didn't hear from me,' she ventured.

'Devastated.' His expression was uncompromisingly hostile.

'That's awful. I wish I'd known.' She leaned forward earnestly. 'But you've heard my explanation. You must understand that I wouldn't want to hurt him for the world.'

She took a sip of the surprisingly refreshing tea and

looked at him over the rim of her cup. He seemed to be having a mental struggle over something. Hopefully she was coaxing him round.

'He's been through a lot recently. I won't let *anyone* disturb his peace of mind,' he stated flatly. 'Your rejection—'

'But I *didn't* reject him!' she cried in frustration.

'He thinks you did.' Stern and forbidding, he leaned forwards. 'I'll find you some snapshots of him to take away. Don't give yourself grief by pursuing this. He won't see you. Accept that and get on with your life.'

'I can't!' she persisted. 'He's only upset because he was hurt when he didn't hear from me. When he knows what happened—'

'He won't hear about it because I'm not telling him your story. Frankly, I just don't believe that you answered him straight away.'

Incensed, she jumped up. 'Then I'll go look for him and tell him myself!'

His arm snaked out to stop her and he rose in one swift and graceful movement, coming to stand menacingly in front of her.

'And I will be forced to prevent you,' he said, very softly.

Jodie squeezed her eyes tightly, to prevent herself from crying in sheer helplessness.

'Please hear me out!' she begged, opening her eyes and staring miserably at his blurred face.

There was a long pause. She stopped breathing. She could hear his breath rasping loudly, feel it hot and quick on her mouth.

'I'll listen,' he muttered. 'But that's all. Sit down. Sell yourself to me if you must.'

She sank gratefully into the seat. A brief reprieve. The

next few minutes were crucial. Feeling oddly hot and flustered, she began to tremble.

'You're…being protective,' she began croakily. 'I understand that. It's good to know someone's been looking out for him. But, like you, I swear I only want what's best for him.'

He grunted and slanted her a cynical glance. 'I wonder. Would you surrender your own needs for his?'

'Can you explain that remark?' she asked in a guarded tone.

'If you really cared for him,' he said quietly, 'you'd do what was in his best interests, not yours.'

She raised one eyebrow. 'And his best interests are…?' He didn't answer and dropped his gaze with a frown. Jodie felt a spurt of hope. 'You're not sure, are you?' she cried shakily. 'He's insisting that he doesn't want to see me—and you're now wondering if he's making a mistake! Morgan, think about this! You can't in all decency stand between us! You'd have it on your conscience all your life if you didn't at least try to persuade him to change his mind! You know that. I can see it in your face. Oh, please give me a chance!'

Morgan drew in a long, hard breath, his eyes betraying the doubts in his mind. Jodie's pulses raced and she twisted her hands together nervously.

'I need some time to think about it,' he growled.

She beamed in delight. 'That's wonderful! Thank you!' she cried passionately.

'I'm only taking time to consider the situation. Nothing's fundamentally changed. Don't build up your hopes,' Morgan warned.

She flung back her head and laughed, her eyes sparkling. 'I'm an optimist. I have to hope! I want to hold my own father in my arms so much that I ache with longing!'

'Then protect yourself from that hope. You could be badly hurt if I decide you must not see him,' he said, his voice low and thick.

Jodie felt a tremor run right through her body. 'It would break my heart,' she breathed.

'Better than you breaking his,' Morgan observed.

'But…why would I?' she asked, bewildered. 'How could I?'

'Do you know anything about him?' he shot.

'No, nothing! That's what's so awful—'

'You know he lives in a large house,' he pointed out cynically.

She drew herself up, insulted by the implication. 'You think I care about his money? That's not why I came! If you can't identify truth and honesty and real affection when you hear it, then I feel sorry for you!'

His eyes flickered. 'You're making it very difficult for me, Jodie,' he said, almost to himself.

She bit her lip, hardly able to bear the suspense which hung in the air between them so tautly she thought it almost crackled with tension. He seemed unable to tear his gaze away from her—and she found herself locked in his thrall.

'Just…what is your connection with him?' she asked, sobered by the power he could wield over her future.

'I'm his right-hand man. He trusts me and my judgement.' The dark eyes continued to bore remorselessly into hers.

She gulped, her head swimming. Tiredness. She had to push this on. 'You could sway him, then?' she said with difficulty.

'If I wanted.'

'Please want!' she pleaded.

He jerked back a little, as if startled by what she'd said.

There was a brief, hot melting of that intent gaze and she felt that at last she was getting somewhere.

He wasn't as hostile. A faint warmth was emanating from him, an imperceptible softening of his hard-hewn face as he contemplated her, weighing her up, assessing everything about her.

She flushed, her mouth drying as his thick lashes fluttered and his downward gaze wandered to her bare throat, her breasts, and then to her legs, which she'd hooked over one another. She wanted to tug down the suddenly embarrassing short skirt to hide an inch or two of slender thigh, but that would have drawn attention there.

And now he was studying her parted lips, and she could actually feel them plumping up in some odd biological response. Hastily she sipped her tea, to occupy her wayward mouth and to avoid his scrutiny.

'I stick to the bargain,' he said huskily. 'Try convincing me some more.'

She moistened her lips again before starting. 'I'm twenty-four. I've spent all my working life in an advertising agency where I was on promotions. It was my job to persuade clients in any way I could to take up our ad campaigns—'

'I bet you were very good at your job,' he said, a curl of amusement lifting the corner of his craggy mouth.

'I was!' She furrowed her brow. 'What else? I help two evenings a week at the retirement home nearby—'

'Oh, please!' he mocked. 'You're going too far—'

'It's true!' she said indignantly. 'I'll give you the phone number and you can check!'

'I'll do that.'

'Good—'

'I suppose you're kind to children and animals?' he drawled.

'No, at every opportunity I boil them up in oil—what do you *think?*' she cried crossly. 'I'm just an ordinary sort of person who tries to keep on the straight and narrow and live a decent life—'

'Not that ordinary. You have a boyfriend?'

'Is that relevant?' she asked in surprise.

'Could be,' came the enigmatic answer.

She shrugged. OK, so be it. She'd tell him her bust size and weight if it helped her cause.

'The answer's no. I've just dumped him,' she said with a grimace. 'He was an arrogant controller who'd tried to mould me into his version of the perfect woman!' Her mouth quirked at his raised eyebrow.

'Did he fail?' Morgan asked, clearly doing his best to hide his amusement.

'Dismally. My problem is that I'm highly allergic to thongs!' she said with a giggle.

As she'd expected, he did a double-take, and for a second or two she thought his eyes showed a flicker of genuine interest. Then the impenetrable shutters came down again.

'So when your relationship broke up,' he drawled, 'you decided to give your father in England a whirl, for want of something better?'

'No! It wasn't like that at all!' she said, bristling. 'Hearing from my father was the catalyst for change. My boyfriend's attitude to a reunion with my father was unsympathetic and obstructive. OK, I took my time realising this, but eventually I did—and saw my boyfriend for what he was. A selfish, manipulative, bullying brute!' She pinned Morgan with a determined stare. 'I've spent the last seven years being walked over. I won't be pushed around any more—not by anyone,' she said meaningfully.

'I think you've made that apparent,' he murmured.

Had she gone too far? She looked at him edgily. 'So what's your verdict?'

'The jury's out,' he drawled.

A sudden feeling of hopelessness washed over her. He was playing with her, leading her on. Fatigue and disappointment made her limbs leaden and her brain ragged as she tried to keep up the pressure on him.

'Look. I'm shattered. I haven't the energy to joust with you but I am desperate to see my father,' she said, her voice cracking with emotion. 'If it makes it any easier for you, I totally understand that if he eventually decides that he wants to live his life without me—then that's his choice to make and I will have to accept his decision.'

Morgan nodded in approval. 'Good! That's settled, then,' he murmured with satisfaction.

She saw tension ease from him and felt her own nerves tighten. It looked as if he was going to send her away with a flea in her ear! Annoyed, she fixed him with her brilliant green eyes and grimly set about persuading him to plead on her behalf.

'However,' she said sweetly, 'I'm sure you'll agree that it should be *his* decision, based on personal knowledge of me. It would be wrong if he didn't even see me face-to-face, so that I could explain that there might have been a mix-up with the mail,' she added, being generous about her suspicions concerning Morgan's part in the 'mix-up'.

'He still might not believe you,' he suggested cynically.

'Oh, yes, he would! He'd look into my eyes and find the truth there!' she insisted stubbornly, passion pouring from her blazing eyes. 'You have seen his letter and read his sentiments. He must still care about me deep down! I'm convinced he'll be overjoyed that I've turned up! You may not have read enough of his letter to me to know that he mentioned he'd just moved house—and that he had something special to tell me. I've been consumed with curiosity ever since. You can't deny me the right to see my own father, not when he was initially so anxious that we should be reunited! He must want me, mustn't he?'

Morgan scowled at his tea. His mouth tightened and then he gave a small exhalation of breath. Jodie waited, tense with anticipation.

'Perhaps,' he hedged reluctantly.

Jodie gasped and clasped her hands in delight, drawing his dark, assessing gaze. 'So I'm close to passing muster?' she asked with a relieved laugh, her eyes spangled with deep jade lights.

'You're persuasive,' was all he'd say.

It was enough for her. The moment had come! She jumped up eagerly. 'Let me ask him! Lead me to him! I just can't wait any longer, Morgan. I'll burst if you keep me dangling in suspense!'

He shifted uncomfortably. 'It's…not that simple—'

'Why not?' she cried in exasperation.

He leant back in his chair, studying her expressionlessly. 'He's not here.'

Jodie's jaw dropped in dismay and she gave a little gasp of disappointment.

'Not…*here*! But I imagined…hoped… Oh, when's he coming back?' she wailed.

'Not…today,' he dissembled.

She slumped back into the chair, totally depressed. 'None of this is working out as I expected,' she said morosely. 'This means I'll have to get back into that wretched car, battle my way along the wrong side of the road and search for the hotel.' Her head lolled back and she heaved a heavy sigh. 'It's not a prospect I relish. I feel shattered. I've been living on adrenaline for days. You can't have any idea what this meeting means to me, Morgan!'

'Have a piece of cake,' he suggested gruffly.

'Keep my strength up?' Dejectedly she took the plate and picked at the fruit cake in a desultory fashion as her thoughts came tumbling out. 'It's my fault, I suppose,' she mused. 'I should have waited for a reply to the recorded delivery. But I was mad keen to see him.' She met his gaze, her eyes clouded with sadness.

'Why is it so important to you?' he asked quietly.

'Because he's the only family I've got now. He and my mother separated when I was a year old. Mom and her boyfriend took me to New York and we lost touch with my father. Mom died when I was six—'

'Your mother is *dead*?' he broke in sharply.

'Yes,' she replied, too engrossed in her own problems to pay much attention to his alerted state.

'God!' he groaned. 'Eighteen years ago! If only Sam had known!'

A film of tears washed over her eyes at the implication that her father would have contacted her sooner.

'Mom wasn't much of a mother, but she was better than my foster-parents. All this time I thought I had no living relative in the whole world! W-when my f-father wrote—' She broke off, a lump filling her throat.

'I don't need to hear this,' Morgan rasped.

'You do!' she cried passionately, her eyes glistening with unshed tears. 'I want you to know what this means to me! I discovered that my father was *alive*! It was the most wonderful present I could ever have been given. He was in England, walking, breathing, sleeping... I couldn't think straight. I went around the apartment in a daze, bursting into song...'

Unable to stop herself, she flung her arms in the air in an impassioned gesture as she relived those first joyful hours. His eyes flickered with a strange, glittering light and she faltered, bringing her arms down quickly, lest he think she was mad. But he had to know the intensity of her feelings!

'Morgan,' she explained fervently, 'you had to be there to see me! I danced, I hugged myself breathless, ate a whole tub of ice cream...! Oh,' she cried, husky with the memory, 'I was so happy I felt delirious. I grinned at everyone I met. New York reeled! For days I walked on air—and then every so often I'd burst into tears. I felt so far away from him, you see.'

There was a long silence. Morgan seemed to be finding it difficult to speak. Once again, tension spun a thick blanket between them, crushing the air from her lungs. Jodie clasped her hands anxiously, scanning his face. Her heart turned over. Something was wrong!

Numbed by Morgan's look of pity, she waited, a prey to her imagination. Her father was dead, she thought immediately, her eyes rounding in horror!

'Look...you mustn't get your hopes up. You can't see him now, or in the foreseeable future.'

She blinked, trying to puzzle this out. 'Why?' she asked, her face pale.

The breath caught sharply in her throat. Something akin to anguish had slashed across his well-deep eyes before vanishing again. But it was obvious to Jodie that he was profoundly disturbed about something. She noticed that he'd clenched his jaw hard and balled his hands into fists till the bone shone white through the skin over his knuckles.

Her pulses went into overdrive as fear skittered through her. Her cup clattered to the saucer, freed unwittingly from her jittery fingers. Tea spilled across the blue check tablecloth but neither of them gave the stain more than a cursory glance.

'My father...? He's not...not...?' she whispered desperately, and choked on the terrible lump which blocked her throat.

'No!' Morgan cried quickly, interpreting her distress. 'He's not dead! I didn't mean that!'

In a surprising, reassuring gesture, his hand reached out to hers and held it tightly when she let out a small groan of relief.

'What, then?' she breathed.

'He's unwell—in hospital,' Morgan replied, sounding strained. 'He's been ill for some time—'

Jodie trembled. 'Was…was he ill when he wrote to me?' she asked in a small voice. 'He sounded idyllically happy—'

'He was—but his health was poor even then. That's partly why he contacted you. And now…' His jaw tightened. 'I have to tell you that he's taken a severe turn for the worse—'

'What do you mean?' She stared, aghast, her eyes wide and horrified. 'How much…worse is he?' she croaked. Breaking free, she leapt to her feet in agitation. 'Tell me the truth. I must know!' she demanded hysterically.

His mouth became grim. 'You need to sit down—'

'Answer me! I want to know!' she wailed, ignoring his suggestion.

'Very well. The stark truth. He has pneumonia,' Morgan said quietly. 'He's fighting for his life.'

It was his pained whisper which drained all her body of its strength. The stark gravity of his expression told her—far more than his words—that her father's condition was perhaps more serious than he was letting on.

Stunned by this unexpected development, she swayed as the room whirled around her and a roaring in her ears drowned out anything else he might have said.

With a feeble moan she grabbed weakly at something,

anything, found the chair and collapsed into it, her mind in turmoil.

'No! *No!*' she moaned.

Hot, stinging tears welled from her eyes and poured unchecked down her face. Distraught, shocked beyond belief, she hugged her arms around herself and rocked back and forth, weeping without restraint.

So near and yet so far.

She could have been here months ago! But Chas had told her he couldn't release her from work to go to England. And then there'd been the failure in the mail service—or, worse, Morgan had blocked her letters! And Chas had persuaded her that her father hadn't replied because he'd had second thoughts...

She groaned. All this time she could have been comforting her father, getting to know him, fussing over him... And now he might be close to death.

'Oh, God! My poor father! I—I didn't expect any...anything l-like this!' she mumbled raggedly through her sobs.

The soft folds of a handkerchief touched her hand. She snatched it and pressed the linen against her tear-stained face. He could have caused this situation. She scrubbed her eyes hard and looked at him accusingly.

'I have to ask you this—did...did you hide m-my letters?' she asked bluntly.

'No!' he answered, obviously shocked by the suggestion. 'I couldn't have. I only came to live here a few weeks ago!'

She took a huge, shuddering breath. Her letters had gone astray, then. No wonder Morgan had been so hostile. He'd known that her sick father had written to her, knew how vital it was that she should reply. When no answer had come, Morgan and her father must have hated her for being callous and unfeeling.

She groaned with frustration. But she did care! More than she'd known, more than she could have ever believed! To get so close to being reunited—and then to have that longed-for moment cruelly snatched away—was a worse blow than anything she'd ever known.

This had been her chance to love and be loved unconditionally. To know the purest, most lasting love between a parent and a child.

Her poor father. Dangerously ill…she thought numbly. Her leaden arms dropped and came to rest on the table. She bent her head, too shattered to hold it up any more, and her burning wet cheek found comfort in the soft fabric of her jacket sleeve. Her sobs racked her body till her ribs ached and her throat felt raw.

Dimly, somewhere in the background, she registered an odd crackle, as if someone was brushing a hand across a microphone.

'Excuse me. I have to go!' Morgan muttered.

His chair scraped hastily back and she heard his brisk footsteps crossing the tiled floor rapidly, as though her tears irritated him and he couldn't wait to get out of the room.

Miserably she lifted her head a fraction, suddenly wanting the company of someone, anyone.

'Don't!' she sobbed. But his blurred image was already disappearing through the door.

Her lip trembled uncontrollably. He wasn't giving her the benefit of the doubt. He believed she was a liar and blamed her for upsetting a seriously ill man.

He knew Sam. Cared about him. But she was part of Sam too! She was upset and alone and in a strange country. He *knew* how she felt about seeing her father!

How could he walk out on her? Maybe he was upset himself. But didn't he feel anything for her own grief? She banged her fists on the table. Why were so many men so utterly selfish? *Why* didn't they feel the hurt of others?

A flood of anger and resentment welled up like bitter bile in her mouth and she began to sob as if her heart would break, crying for her father and for herself, hating the cold-hearted Morgan and his lack of humanity.

Her misery intensified. Now she knew where she stood. Entirely alone.

How he'd got out of the kitchen he didn't know. He stuffed the portable baby alarm deeper into his pocket, ravaged by the rawest of emotions.

It had been worse than he'd imagined.

He'd grabbed a bottle from the fridge and picked up the automatic bottle-warmer; grimly he took them to the drawing room, where Jack lay in the rocker-seat uttering plaintive squeaks of protest.

'You pick your moments,' he said quietly. 'Hold on. Just need to plug in this...then we'll undo these straps and you're safe, here with me...'

How safe? came that insistent voice again. When you're tussling with your conscience, toying with the idea that this woman should take her rightful place in this family? When you're close to deliberately handing over your own flesh and blood to a total stranger?

Morgan ground his teeth together, ignoring the maelstrom of his mind, walking up and down with Jack, soothing him with his voice and trying to regain his own equilibrium.

'Hush, little man. Nearly ready,' he muttered. He bent his head and put his cheek to Jack's, desperate for human contact. 'This is tearing me to pieces,' he said bitterly. 'Sam, you, her...'

His brows met in a deep frown as he reined in his ragged thoughts. He didn't want to go through anything like the last few minutes ever again. Jodie's heart-rending sobs had torn through all his defences, getting under his skin more than he could have believed possible.

He should never have asked her in. Damn his sense of morality and fair play! Listening to her had been fatal. She came over as vulnerable, too open and trusting for her own good. Or was she? He'd been fooled before. Badly.

He frowned, feeling keenly his past failure to protect Sam. The repercussions had been disastrous. A shudder of anger and repulsion ran through him. That meant he must do everything in his power to ensure that this woman wouldn't hurt Sam in any way whatsoever.

Jodie was a mass of contradictions: brightly dressed and assertive, yet emotional and sensitive. Morgan grunted. Fascinating she might be, but that could be a deadly combination for a sick man who needed peace and a hassle-free life.

It was essential that he kept a clear head to deal with the threat she posed. Common sense told him to get rid of her. Yet his own innate sense of decency and compassion kept getting in the way.

And, aching with his own anguish about Sam, he'd found himself on the brink of taking that shaking, slender body in his arms and holding her close to show that he shared and sympathised with her grief.

Only his fear for Jack's future had stopped him, urging caution instead of a knee-jerk emotional response.

'All ready now,' he murmured lovingly to the baby. 'There. Worth waiting for, wasn't it? Such big tears...'

His head lifted, his eyes dark with the torment of the past. He'd witnessed hysterical weeping just like Jodie's not long ago, when Teresa had begged him to remain silent about who had fathered her baby. He'd made a promise to a dying woman out of pity, to give her peace of mind. And to protect Sam.

From then on he'd been floundering in an unfamiliar mire of lies and deceit. His mouth tightened in resolve. He'd never go down that road again.

He stared at Jack's small, intent face as he drowsily suckled. Blissful innocence. Heart-wrenching defencelessness... He could never part with this precious gift, this child—*his* child!

'She could take you away from me!' he said to Jack, his eyes blazing and his heart pounding violently in his chest at the very thought. 'I won't ever let that happen!' he vowed fervently.

Whether she was needy or not, he had to persuade her to abandon any ideas of a cosy reunion. But he felt a heel for doing so. Even though he was doing exactly what Sam wanted. The older man had said emphatically—almost hysterically—that he didn't want anything to do with her.

However, Morgan wasn't comfortable with the decision he had now made—even though it meant that his own future with his son would be assured.

The problem was that it would be tough as hell seeing Jodie walk away unsatisfied, knowing how badly she yearned for her father.

He raked a hand through his hair. Curse her for complicating his life!

Jack stopped feeding. With great gentleness Morgan put the baby over his shoulder to burp him. Then he tenderly wiped away the dribble of milk around the petal mouth—and groaned when he incidentally caught a glimpse of his watch as he did so.

'Damn!' he muttered irritably. 'Later than I thought!'

Jodie's arrival had disrupted his plans. The chores would have to wait. Time to leave for the hospital.

On autopilot, he changed Jack's nappy, then found a warm wool hat in the changing bag and carefully pulled it over the thatch of fine black hair before beginning the familiar struggle: getting two small and uncooperative arms into the cosy coat.

And now he had to tell Jodie his decision.

'Hang on a minute,' he said softly, tucking the cooing Jack safely into the rocker chair. 'Back soon.'

He pocketed the alarm and set off for the kitchen, dreading the next few minutes. But he found her sprawled across the table fast asleep, her head on her arms.

He stood there for a moment looking at her, his gaze transfixed by the way her gleaming hair hung around her head like a glossy cap and how it shone with rich red colours in the fluorescent light.

Gently he shook her shoulder. It felt fragile beneath the spread of his fingers and his fingers briefly splayed out, recording the delicate bones beneath the warm flesh. Vulnerable, he thought. Despite her bravado. And a twinge of something inexplicable ground through his stomach before he scowled and paid attention to what he had to do.

'Jodie. Jodie!' he said urgently, determined to get this over and done with.

She muttered, but was too deeply asleep to be roused. Sliding his fingers down the sleeve of her jacket, he found that it was wet with tears. An unwanted rogue sympathy dangerously softened his heart.

Without knowing why, he lifted silken strands of hair and tucked them behind her ear so he could see her face. The huge, soulful eyes were thankfully hidden from view, but the sight of her cutely curling wet lashes touched his emotions.

With a groan, he caught her chin gently in one hand. 'Jodie!'

Her head lolled heavily and he muttered with exasperation, conscious that time was ticking away. She was out like a light.

Well, she couldn't stay there. And he couldn't hang about waiting for her to wake up. Nothing for it, then.

He slid a hand beneath her and lifted. She snuggled with annoying trust in his arms, her head burrowing a little place for itself in his neck—just like Jack did. Her breath came soft and even on his throat. Combined with the feel of her plush curves and the sweet scent of her hair, it was a heady sensation.

An undeniable hunger began to lap at his body. He recognised it as the long-denied desire for the softness of a woman, the sensual pleasure of exploring a woman's body, the release of tightly controlled passions and the tender aftermath.

He scowled. And what had all that cost him in the past?

Angrily he strode out and climbed the stairs. Surrendering anything to a woman had a price. If you made a mistake—and he'd made one too many—you went through hell.

It wasn't particularly surprising that he was reacting to this sexy and appealing woman. He'd been celibate for a long time and every blink of those incredible eyes had sent tingles through him, invigorating each cell in his body. But he could handle that...

Morgan's muscles contracted, proving the opposite. She'd wriggled, and the pressure of her breasts against his chest was fast eroding his resolve. Tight-lipped, he placed her on the four-poster bed in the guest room and eased her arms from around his neck.

For a moment her face lifted and their mouths were close. She sighed, and the urge to kiss those moist, parted lips almost overcame him.

Somehow he drew back and busied himself with briskly hauling the duvet out of the linen press. He hesitated. She'd been travelling for hours. She'd probably sleep through the evening and into the night.

His dark eyes flickered over the thigh boots. Hesitantly he slid his hand over the soft suede and took the zip tab between finger and thumb. In doing so his hand brushed against firm, warm flesh, but he conquered the tremor which slid with a languid warmth through his body and eased the boots off.

Nothing to it. Ignoring the long expanses of shapely leg, he considered the jacket. It had to come off too. Rolling her over on one side and then the other, he finally managed this.

Her arm came up and twined around his neck, pulling his head down to her breast with surprising strength. He found that his face was nestling luxuriantly in the folds of silk, the rise and fall of her perfumed breasts making his head swim. He stayed there for only a split second but it was almost too long.

With ruthless will he extricated himself and hastily covered her with the duvet, bringing it safely up to her chin, as if he knew he had to obliterate all sight, all memory of that delicious, tempting body.

Her cheeks were streaked with tears, her lashes still spiky. In a moment of madness he thought of washing her face with warm water, but he realised he must stay away from this woman and banish her from every part of him.

She was Sam's daughter. Hadn't he caused enough trouble with Sam's mistress already?

He was playing with fire by finding Jodie sexually desirable. Merciless with himself, he drew the curtains around the bed and left her a note in case she woke up, saying he would be out for a couple of hours or so.

And then he showered—cold, invigorating, beneficial—shaved and dressed, collected Jack and headed for the hospital, preparing himself for the harrowing sight of his dearly loved Sam fighting for breath, for life itself.

CHAPTER FOUR

JODIE stirred, her deep, dreamless sleep interrupted by a low rumbling. Groggy and barely conscious, she forced her heavy eyes to open a fraction. Her half-conscious mind took in the swirling greyness above—where she would have expected the darkness of a ceiling—and raw instinct took over.

'Fire!' she yelled, terrified, yet too drugged from the depths of sleep to think straight. 'Help! Fire!'

Her eyes stubbornly refused to focus. A numbing lethargy had taken over her limbs, demanding that she fall asleep again. A nightmare, she told herself hazily.

Smoke surrounded her. Bedding had wrapped itself around her legs, preventing her from escaping. In her dream, or waking, she screamed in panic and forced herself to fight for release, blindly lashing out at everything in her way.

'Help! Help me!' she whimpered as the danger became clear. And then to her utter relief she felt cool air on her face and body as the duvet slid away.

The smoke parted. There was blackness beyond. Paralysed with fear, she blinked in confusion, her eyes thick and heavy, and her tongue cleaving to the roof of her mouth. A shadowy figure moved into sight and she raked in a strangled breath, her eyes wide with horror.

'Hush! It's all right.'

A hand rested comfortingly on her bare shoulder and a light snapped on from somewhere behind her head. She found herself staring into Morgan's liquid dark eyes. They were soft and molten and she felt instantly overwhelmed with relief.

'Fire!' she husked.

'There is...no fire,' he breathed.

'There was...smoke!' she mumbled foggily, trying to make her comatose brain work.

'Uhuh. A...dream,' he said hoarsely.

'No—I heard a rumbling, burning, perhaps...' Her voice faded. There was no smell of smoke, no sign of it. 'I did see smoke!' she insisted, afraid he'd think she was mad. 'I opened my eyes and saw it...'

'You couldn't have,' he interrupted sharply, bending down to pick up the duvet.

She felt its warmth suddenly descending on the bare skin of her pelvis, hips and legs, where previously there had been nothing. Shocked, she realised that she was still wearing her skirt—and that it had ridden up to her waist in her struggles.

She gasped. That meant that when Morgan had first switched on the light... Oh, sweet heaven! Her citrus silk briefs, her bare stomach and thighs and the lace-topped hold-ups would have been exposed to his penetrating gaze!

Furtively she wriggled the skirt down and tentatively moved her hands up her body. Her cheeks flamed when her fingers encountered the soft nakedness of one breast. It seemed her T-shirt had behaved just as recklessly!

Appalled, she cringed beneath the duvet, her apprehensive eyes flicking up to his. He looked as indifferent and as grim-faced as ever, his jaw clenched hard as hewn granite.

He hadn't been interested, she thought, and frowned, shocked by her indignation. Yet she didn't want men to make passes at her as if she were some sex object. She wanted to be loved for her whole self. So why should she be annoyed?

'Relax,' Morgan clipped. 'You're safe.'

With difficulty she hauled her mind back. 'But if I didn't see smoke, what did I see?' she muttered crossly.

'You're in a four-poster bed,' he explained. 'Look up.'

Her sulky gaze followed his. She saw a dove-grey canopy above and its swirling pattern—like smoke. Curtains of the same material had been drawn around the sides. That was what she'd seen surrounding her in the darkness. She'd been scared of grey fabric!

'Ohhh!' she groaned. Keeping the duvet safely up to her neck, she collapsed back on the pillows, deeply embarrassed. 'I feel so stupid. I'm terribly sorry,' she mumbled in contrition. 'I was deeply asleep. My brain must have picked up a couple of clues and gone into survival mode.'

'It wasn't your fault. You didn't know where you were,' he agreed in a faintly slurred voice.

It was then that she registered that he was wearing a white towelling robe, open at the throat and chest and loosely tied at the waist. It was short enough to reveal strong, sinewy legs and a glimpse of muscular thigh.

He'd been in bed. Or in the bath. Were those beads of sweat on his forehead or dampness? Jodie realised she was staring and said hurriedly, 'What's the time?' She peered at her watch on the bedside table and groaned in dismay. 'It's five a.m.! How awful! I woke you!' Her hot, apologetic face lifted earnestly to his.

'I was already awake,' he replied. 'I was doing the washing.'

Her eyes rounded. *'Washing?'* and then it dawned on her. 'That explains it!' she cried. 'The spin cycle—it must have woken me!'

'Then it's for me to apologise to you,' he said quietly. 'If you're all right now, then—'

'Wait a minute!' Jodie was frowning, trying to piece together what had happened. 'I don't recall going to bed. I'm...I'm still wearing my clothes...but not...all of them... Did I...? Who...?'

She gulped, frightened that so many hours could be a complete blank, her anxious, wide eyes meeting his in a silent question.

'You cried yourself to sleep at the kitchen table.'

She remembered that. Her eyes narrowed at his flat, unemotional delivery. He really didn't give a damn about her!

'It's hardly surprising!' she said feistily. 'And...then?' she queried, feeling herself tense up in anticipation.

He scowled. 'You couldn't stay slumped awkwardly over the table all night...'

His tone was matter-of-fact and curt, but he was strung taut, every muscle in his body straining so much that he shook imperceptibly. Jodie gloomily realised that he must be thoroughly irritated with her. He'd even checked himself in mid-sentence, almost as if he couldn't be bothered to waste his time continuing.

'So?' she prompted with a glower, needing to hear from his own lips what had happened.

'Obvious. I carried you up here,' he clipped.

Like a sack of potatoes, apparently, she thought grumpily. 'Well, thank you,' she muttered, remembering her manners.

He shrugged his wide shoulders as if it were all in a day's work—and an unpleasant job, at that.

'Had to be done.'

The insult to her feminine pride cut her to the quick. But then she found herself consumed with the image of herself, curled up in his arms, the subject of his inscrutable gaze.

At some stage he must have removed her boots. And her jacket. Her tongue flickered across dry lips and they parted as she drew in her breath. Even though he wasn't interested in her as a woman, she found the situation uncomfortably intimate. And alarmingly arousing.

'You—you were very kind to let me stay the night,' she said throatily, frowning at the treacle-like thickness of her speech. She must be more tired than she'd known.

His eyes glittered, then his dark lashes lowered to conceal them. 'I didn't have any choice,' he growled, so quietly that she barely heard at all.

And in the crushing silence that fell she became very aware of everything about him. Suddenly his mouth seemed more carnal, its lines curving with a beautiful sensuality. Her lips parted. He was clean-shaven now, and she found herself aching to touch the smooth lines of his angular jaw.

Her eyes half closed. Not from drowsiness, but from an unstoppable surge of sexual awakening which made her feel she was swimming through warm seas, every part of her body invaded by a lethargic heat.

She'd never felt like this before. Not this desperate, inescapable and reckless need to be touched, to touch...

She swallowed, bewildered and appalled by her uncontrollable lust. It was driving her into danger. This man would take no prisoners.

'Goodnight, then,' she managed, brutally denying her basic instincts.

''Night!' he shot back through his teeth.

He pulled the curtains across and left before she could hold him there any longer. But as he thundered angrily down the stairs he knew with a heart-stopping shock that she had captured a part of him already.

He groaned. Every inch of his body was threatening mutiny. It clamoured to be free of the rigid control he was imposing on it.

The blood was still pumping in his veins, red and hot. The breath had been rasping in his throat so loudly he'd been sure she'd comment on his laboured intake. His eyes could only stare, his lips part in readiness. His hands had almost reached out and touched...

He sucked in a harsh breath, his mind seeing nothing but the sweet curve of her hips, the dark, triangular shadow beneath the tantalisingly fragile scrap of acid-yellow silk. And then that smooth softness of her thighs above the lacy stockings. The incredible swell of her milky-white breast with its dark plum centre, tantalisingly sleepy and unawoken...

He'd longed to bring it to life. To surround it with his mouth, pulling gently till it peaked hard and sweet while he caressed her fabulous body, feeling its flawless silk against his flesh and bone, crushing her to him till they melted in heat and desire...

That was how he'd felt. His need had been so unexpected and fierce that it had stunned him. And he'd stood there helplessly, a martyr to his lust and shaking with pent-up desire, disgusted that he should feel like this about a total stranger. Sam's daughter. It was a direct betrayal of Sam's trust. Again.

Ruthlessly he'd suppressed his primal urges. And so he'd parried her remarks, calmed her fears, and had somehow walked away without making a total prat of himself.

'Hell!' he muttered.

Every male instinct in his screaming body had demanded that he should put his arms around her, comfort her, allow that to lead to a gentle kiss, and slowly, tenderly make love to her before he lost his reason.

'God!' he breathed, walking unsteadily into the kitchen.

This was an extra complication he could never have foreseen!

Shaking with the effort of containing every rampaging pagan impulse in his protesting body, he made himself a pot of coffee and concentrated with ferocious intent on the expulsion of the luscious Jodie from his mind.

Jodie lay on the bed horribly wide awake and wishing that the aching emptiness in her body would go. Restless, she slipped out of bed, intending to find her nightdress in the case she'd noticed by the dressing table.

Instead, she paused in front of the mirror and took a good, hard look at herself: a tousled, wide-eyed wanton. She was astonished by the change in her appearance. Where had this pouting-lipped seductive hoyden come from?

'The last thing you need,' she told herself crossly, 'is a selfish, hard-bitten guy who wouldn't know what tenderness was if it socked him in the eye twice a day!'

Her stomach rumbled suddenly. She needed food. It must be hours and hours since she'd last eaten. Planning on sneaking down to the kitchen, she dived for her case, rummaging around inside it and bringing out a pair of soft jersey palazzo pants and a warm sweatshirt.

Chas had said she was highly sexed, she mused soberly, changing into the banana-yellow outfit. Although if she was honest it had always been the triumph of hope over experience. Chas had never satisfied her.

Twisting a red and lemon scarf in her hair, she paused, her eyes rounding in alarm. Maybe that was the trouble—she was one of those women who were insatiable, who needed sex like some people needed lunch, and then second helpings, please! The thought was mortifying.

Granted, Morgan was the hunkiest guy she'd ever met, that dark intractable manner only adding to her fatal fascination—but she'd promised herself that she would find someone who was gentle and kind, full of consideration for others. Someone who utterly adored her. Less than that she would not accept. And in any case, she had something more important on her mind.

She sighed heavily, realising she was no nearer to seeing her father. She was even more determined now that she knew he was ill. Morgan *had* to give her the name of the hospital. She'd get it out of him at breakfast time if she had to lick his boots in the process!

Halfway across the landing, she stopped in her tracks. She'd see him sooner than that—Morgan had said he was doing the washing! If she went down now, she'd bump into him! Her face coloured with embarrassment. For a fraction of a second she almost chickened out, and then impatiently brushed away her sense of discomfiture.

She needed food and this was her opportunity to pin him down. *Without fail.*

He was struggling to fold a damp sheet when she padded into the kitchen, her bare feet silent on the terracotta tiles. She took one look at his brooding face and powerful figure and her stomach swooped.

'I'm starving,' she announced as a diversionary tactic for her runaway carnal impulses.

He turned, frowned in the general direction of her searing yellow outfit, and continued battling with the sheet.

'Eggs and bacon in the fridge.'

''Fraid I'm hopeless at cooking,' she admitted. 'I was thinking of toast and coffee, and perhaps a fruit pie or a chocolate cake—'

'In the larder.'

His head jerked abruptly to indicate where. The sheet slipped from his fingers and he glared at it, then her, as if it were her fault.

The old Jodie would have crumpled. This one said drily, 'Here. I'll help you with that.'

They did sides to middle and end to end. The moment she began walking towards him with her end of the sheet she felt the hairs rise on the back of her neck.

'Thanks,' he said curtly, and seemed as anxious as she was to avoid close contact because he virtually snatched the folded sheet from her fingers and spent a while arranging it over a chrome rail attached to the front of the stove.

She let out a shaky breath. It had happened again! Why, she couldn't imagine. Though…he was a hard, moody man, and handsome enough to give women grief. However, she'd had enough of that. For her, men were as passé as thongs. All she had to do now, she thought ruefully, was convince her hormones.

'I couldn't sleep,' she remarked casually, in an effort to break the tense silence.

'So I see.' He yanked at the tie on his robe, knotting it more securely. It was a telling gesture. One of those indicators like…folding one's arms…which made it plain that he was being defensive. Keep out, it said. Don't invade my territory.

She felt deflated. He didn't feel comfortable with her around. He didn't like her, didn't trust her and couldn't bear to be in the same room. And now he was reinforcing her theory by turning his back on her at every opportunity.

Jodie glared at the broad expanse of white towelling. Her wretched sexual hunger interfered briefly and forced her to admire the shapely triangle of his back and the small waist and hips.

And then she pulled herself together. He had his need to be alone, but *she* needed information. Which she'd get, come hell or high water!

Whirling on her small bare feet, she found the bread, the

butter and a large apple pie, and brought them triumphantly to the table.

'I'll help myself to coffee,' she added, pleased with her assertiveness. Wordlessly he handed her a bone china mug and she filled it to the brim. 'I irritate you, don't I?' she said bluntly.

He gave a small and mirthless laugh, finished stacking wet handkerchiefs on top of the chrome lid which covered a hot plate, then hauled an ironing board out of a cupboard.

'You're a complication,' he acknowledged drily.

At least he was honest. She watched him plug in an iron and grab a shirt from a huge basket of ironing, quite dazzled by his domesticity.

'Why are you doing this?' she asked, unable to hold back her curiosity. 'Don't you have a daily help?'

'I *am* the daily help.'

Her eyes widened in surprise. *'You?'* It briefly crossed her mind that Morgan and her father could be lovers, but the idea was so ridiculous and Morgan so utterly male that she dismissed it immediately. 'Where's the toaster?' she said, looking around for one.

'Here.' He took the bread from her, lifted the other chrome lid on the stove and slid the slices between two pieces of mesh shaped like a tennis racket. 'Keep an eye on that. It toasts very quickly.'

She kept lifting the lid and peering at it. The heat coming off the hot plate was intense, and, as he'd said, the toast was done in a matter of seconds. She wasn't sure what impressed her most, the stove—which seemed to be doubling up as an ironing machine and a clothes dryer—or Morgan's domestic talents.

'Is this is your job, then? Washing and ironing and so on?' she fished, lavishly spreading the butter.

He frowned at her from under his lowered brows and

expertly dealt with the collar, cuffs and the front of the shirt.

'No. I do it because someone has to.'

'At five in the morning?' she murmured in amazement, pushing up her sleeves in the warmth of the kitchen. She sat on the edge of the table eating the toast, her legs swinging, scarlet toenails twinkling in the bright light.

Morgan slanted an odd look at her. 'I can't fit it in otherwise,' he said slowly.

'Why don't you employ someone?'

Tight-lipped at her questioning, he pressed fiercely on the shirt, steam rising in clouds. 'The only two possible daily helps who live locally worked here for a few days and then walked out.'

She wasn't surprised. He'd try anyone's patience. Generously sugaring her coffee, she mused that it was his fault if he had to do his own smalls. So she bit back an urge to offer help and bit into the bread instead, munching away and watching him covertly from under her lashes.

Almost immediately she felt that surge of electricity again, a strong current which seemed to pull her towards him. He must have sensed she was watching him because he flicked a glance at her and stopped his manic ironing while their eyes locked.

Jodie felt her mouth drying. She squirmed, caught helplessly in his magnetic field, the remorseless sexual tension boiling up like a seething cauldron inside her.

She seemed to be all heat, her mind consumed by the sight of Morgan, dark, virile, naked beneath the robe...

Swallowing, furious with herself, she slid shakily off the table and moved further away, wandering about at the far end of the kitchen. It wasn't enough. She was reduced to opening and shutting cupboard doors with her free hand in the effort to dissipate the explosive energy building inside her.

And although the temptation was to stay and drink in Morgan's hot sexuality, she knew she must ask what she needed to know and leave, so that she could escape her own frightening desires and retire to the safety of her room.

'My...father...' she began in a terrible croak, and was forced to moisten her lips. She put down the toast in case he saw how much her hands shook and she pushed them into her pockets, determined to see this through. 'I want to know where he is,' she said jerkily, 'and how he is and when I can see him. I want to know all about him—'

'I visited him yesterday while you were asleep,' he broke in obliquely.

Her huge green eyes flinched at the sight of his grim face. It didn't look as if he had good news. She began to tremble.

'Oh! H-how is he?'

'Stable,' he replied, sounding utterly drained.

'What does "stable" actually mean?' she asked anxiously.

'I believe it means he's not getting any worse.' He picked up another shirt and spread out a sleeve on the ironing board, his movements slow and laboured, as if he was walking through a fog. 'They think he'll pull through,' he said huskily, his voice vibrating with emotion.

'Oh, dear God!'

Overwhelmed by relief, Jodie closed her eyes and let out a whimper. The room seemed to spin around and she would have fallen if he hadn't come quickly to her side and steadied her.

His touch brought her sharply back to reality. With intense clarity she could feel the welcome pressure of his hands around her arms, could trace by feel alone each long finger and its soft pad at the tip. The rise and fall of his breath quickened now, and she inhaled the faint warm aura of his body: a clean, indefinable faint fragrance of fresh soap.

She quivered in the thick silence, struggling to understand why he was shaking too. Apparently her father's illness had hit him hard. Sympathetic tears began to trickle down her face again.

'I don't believe this! What a wimp! I don't *want* to cry!' she mumbled crossly, aware that he was looking at her intently. 'But…it was a shock, hearing that my father was on the danger list, Morgan—and now he's going to be all right, I—I—!'

'Of course. You're letting go. I do understand,' he said quietly.

Something in his tone alerted her. 'You're very fond of him, aren't you?' she asked huskily.

'Fond? I love him,' he replied, his breath warm on her lips.

She stared, surprised by his passion and transfixed by the torment in his eyes until she recalled his Latin American background. He would love and hate with a ferocity she could barely imagine.

'If…if he had died,' she said, stumbling over her words as emotion claimed her, 'I—I couldn't have *borne* it.'

'Neither could I,' he said thickly.

She choked on a sob, her lower lip trembling uncontrollably. Pulling her close, he slid his arms around her comfortingly, and then his hands were stroking her hair so tenderly that she could hardly bear the sweetness of his caress.

He really did care for her father, she thought muzzily. Her cheek lay on the soft lapel of his cotton robe; her lips just touched the hot silk of his chest. She could hear his heart beating loudly and suddenly she knew why he'd been short-tempered and curt with her. He'd been desperately worried, perhaps to the exclusion of everything else.

Without realising it, she nuzzled more trustingly in his arms, musing that there was a special link between Morgan and her father which she'd discover soon. In the meantime, she could almost forgive Morgan for his abruptness.

'It's been hard for you too, hasn't it?' she whispered, guiltily enjoying the feel of her mouth against his skin.

'Harder for him,' he growled.

That touched her. She inhaled a raw breath, her emotions stretched too far in compassion for her father, her own relief, and an overwhelming sympathy for Morgan, who was stoically trying not to let his anxiety get the upper hand.

'It's all right now,' she murmured soothingly. 'He's on the mend. It's wonderful news.'

On an impulse, she hugged him, loving the firmness of his body in the circle of her embrace. And then she lifted her head to look at him, her eyes bright with happiness.

'He'll be back here sooner than you know. Won't that be wonderful?'

She felt his muscles relax, felt the huge outrush of air from his lungs. His cheek came down against hers and her arms tightened around him again in sheer relief. Knots in her slender shoulders unwound as she relaxed completely in his arms.

Her father would be well and Morgan had accepted her. There would be no barriers between them now.

She sighed, a gentle joy easing away the remnants of tension. Her body felt warm and molten against his, almost boneless. Suddenly her chin was being tipped up by a questing finger and she smiled up at him, tears still swilling her bright eyes.

Time seemed to stand still. Her breathing was suspended. She was lost, drowning in the dark pools of his liquid eyes, her lips parting of their own volition as his head angled, the light gleaming with an aching beauty on his raw cheek-bones and sinfully smooth jaw.

She knew she should move, say something, even, but speech and conscious thought had deserted her. An irresistible force was weighting her lids and compelling her eyes to close before she understood why.

And then all reality was obliterated because his mouth was on hers, firm yet gentle, his kiss more sweet and tormenting in its restrained passion than any she'd ever known.

Her head tipped back in abandoned pleasure and she wound her arms around his neck with a little whimper of need. Without any thought to what she was doing, she kissed him back, only knowing that she wanted him to stroke her body, to hold her tightly and to kiss her like this for hour after hour till her blind need to be loved had been sated.

But he broke her dream by gently pushing her back, his hands supporting her as he stared, blinking, at her ecstatic face.

'I think,' he said thickly, 'that we're both overreacting to the news about Sam.'

She stared at him blankly, her lungs almost devoid of breath. For a moment his gaze dropped to her parted lips and she thought—crazily hoped—he was going to kiss her again, but he inhaled sharply.

'Yes,' she agreed reluctantly.

He frowned. 'The two of us have been under some strain. Needed someone to hug...'

She released her grip on his robe, pulled herself together and managed a weak smile, thankful that he was defusing the situation.

'You're right! Lucky the vicar wasn't to hand!' she suggested, unnaturally bright. Slipping away and grabbing a piece of stone-cold toast, she waved it airily to give her time to come up with some coherent reply. 'Relief does the oddest things to people!'

She took a bite at the flaccid bread and wished she hadn't, all the time praying he'd agree and not question why she'd fallen so recklessly into his arms. But since he'd grabbed blindly at the nearest source of comfort, he was clearly ready to believe that was what she'd done too.

'Certainly does. I do apologise. I overstepped the mark.'

Back to his abrupt, clipped self, he took up the ironing again with a grim fervour that astonished her.

'That's OK. Understandable in the circumstances,' she said warmly.

She flashed him a smile but he didn't respond. She sighed with disappointment. She'd been mistaken; he didn't want to unbend towards her. That moment of closeness had been purely a reflex action to her father's improvement.

Her teeth dug into her lower lip. It felt awful, being disliked and thought a liar. If only Morgan would trust her! But at least they'd shared a mutual emotion. That was a start.

'The hospital,' she prompted gently. 'I'd like to ring—'

'No!' he broke in roughly. 'Sam is too ill and too frail to cope with you. He has to concentrate on getting better. I will not allow you near him.'

'But...I thought you might have changed your mind—!' she began in horror.

'Then you're wrong. I have some sympathy for you, but my first duty is to him. He's made his wishes about you quite clear.'

'Based purely on an incorrect assumption about me!' she protested.

'So you claim. It doesn't alter the fact, Jodie, that he doesn't want you. Accept this and—'

'No, I won't!'

'Then you leave me no choice.'

Scowling, he switched off the iron and put it and the board away with a clatter. She was speechless at this turn of events. Avoiding her dismayed gaze, he began to prowl up and down the kitchen.

'My advice,' he went on tightly, 'is that you cut your losses and get on with your life, Jodie. There's nothing here for you, and you'll only give yourself grief by fighting for the *impossible*!'

He had thumped his hand down on the counter angrily, his movements faster and his temper closer to exploding as he stalked up and down the floor like a caged animal.

Jodie gulped. His long legs devoured the length of the kitchen as if he was hungry for a fight, and she cringed back against the stove, the chrome bar biting into her back as she arched away from his unreasonable fury.

'I have to try!' she cried bravely.

He stopped dead, the full force of his wrath turned on her. 'Why do you seem determined to pester a desperately sick man?' he thundered.

'*My father!*' she reminded him hotly.

'Who is in no condition to listen to your excuses—!'

'The truth!' she flared, hands on hips, eyes glittering with combat.

'And who washed his hands of you with the utmost contempt and absolute loathing!' he hurled, white slashes of anger gleaming on his high cheekbones.

Her face paled. 'He doesn't feel that strongly about me...does he?' she moaned, wincing with the pain of what he'd said.

'You drove me to tell you that!' he said in exasperation,

his eyes dark and glittering. He continued his fevered prowling. 'Don't push me any further or you'll regret it! I must protect Sam! He's in no fit state to do so himself!'

'I've *told* you I only want what's best for him!' she protested, frustration making her tearful. She pressed her trembling lips together, her eyes luminous with silent pleading.

'Then go!'

'Not without knowing how he fares! I can't leave. Even if I never see him, I have to know what happens to him—'

'I'll phone you,' he said grimly. 'That's a promise. And now you've taken up enough of my time. I want you out of here—'

'That's rich! I'm his daughter and I have more right to be here than you!' she defended, folding her arms defiantly. 'I'm staying, whatever you say. I will see my father! You can't stop me from enquiring at the hospital about him! If you stand in my way, I'll—I'll call the cops!' she finished wildly.

'Call them!' he snarled, whirling like a cornered tiger. 'They won't be interested. Even if they are, I'll tell them how you broke his heart when you didn't answer his letter, how that had repercussions far beyond anything you could ever imagine—'

'What?' she cried, terrified by his savage fury. Her face went white. 'Morgan! What are you saying?'

He checked himself, his chest heaving in his efforts to contain his anger. 'God!' he muttered, passing a shaking hand through his hair. He looked across at her, his eyes narrowed with pain. 'Forget it!' he ordered.

Jodie stared back, shaking uncontrollably with distress. 'I can't!' she whispered. 'You've said too much.'

His mouth compressed. 'Don't you think I know that? And regret it? Leave it, Jodie! You don't want to know!'

'No,' she mumbled. 'But I must. If I am to understand

the depth of his—and your—hatred for me, I have a right
to be told the whole story.'

There was a flash of grudging admiration in his burning
eyes and she lifted her chin, determined to show him that
she could handle anything he had to reveal to her.

'You insist?' he queried. She nodded and he took several
deep breaths. As if drained by anger, he leaned against the
counter, his expression far away. 'You weren't to know
what damage you'd do, of course,' he said, ominously quiet
after his rage. 'When you turned up on the doorstep un-
expectedly I did everything I could to put you off—'

'I noticed!' she glowered.

'Jodie,' he said softly, 'at the time I thought you had
come here on a casual whim, perhaps eager to cash in on
your father's wealth. It was my intention that you'd go
away virtually unscathed, accepting that your father wasn't
interested in you.'

'Does...does he really hate me?' she asked jerkily.

Morgan's slow nod drew a moan from her. 'I'm sorry
you had to know that,' he said roughly. 'For many reasons,
I wanted you to leave before you learned the consequences
of not replying to Sam's letter. I thought it would be too
cruel.' He hauled in a harsh breath. 'But you had to keep
at me, didn't you?' he flung. 'Like a dog worrying a bone!'

Her hand had flown to her mouth. *'What?'* she cried in
agitation. 'What were the repercussions?!'

Morgan's face twisted in pain. She saw him go pale, saw
the torment in his eyes, the contortion of his mouth, and
she shrank back, wishing she'd never started this, almost
wishing she'd turned around and gone home. She gave a
whimper and his eyes flickered, then focused on her as
though he'd been miles away.

'What,' she repeated in a strangled whisper, 'were the
consequences?'

And he answered, in a pained and inaudible growl, 'The
death of the woman he loved.'

CHAPTER FIVE

SHE choked back a sob of horror, frantic to stay in control and to refute his shocking allegation.

'I can't be held responsible for that! It's…' She sucked in a sharp breath. 'It's a wicked thing to say!'

'But true.' He glanced quickly at his watch and she almost exploded with anger.

'How *dare* you? Forget the time!' she yelled. 'This is important! How am I supposed to have killed someone with the Atlantic Ocean between us? You tell me that! I need to know!' she stormed.

'You failed him when he needed you. Sam had fallen in love,' Morgan began. 'He wanted to get in touch with you because he longed to see you before…' Morgan paused, took a steadying breath, avoiding her eyes as if he couldn't bear to look at her. 'Before he got married,' he continued. 'And to do so he needed your mother's address to arrange a divorce.'

'But…my mother was dead!' Jodie protested.

'I know that—now. That information has come a little too late, though,' Morgan replied.

'I still don't understand.'

'I'm getting there. Unfortunately your father chose not to tell his fiancée that he was still married—'

'Why?' she demanded.

He shrugged. 'Your mother could have been anywhere. It could have taken years to trace her. Sam's fiancée was much younger, and—'

'How much younger?' she interrupted.

71

'Nine years older than me,' he replied, his voice tight and stiff. 'Thirty-six.'

'My father must be around sixty!' she said in astonishment. 'Did she love him?' she probed. 'Really love him?'

'How can I answer that?' he hedged. 'Remember, I wasn't around most of the time. All I know is that she wanted to marry him more than anything in the world and he was desperate to make her his wife. Sam feared he'd lose her if she knew there were complications.'

'If she loved him she would have waited!' Jodie said passionately. Morgan just looked at her. 'She didn't love him! *Did she?*'

His lips compressed. 'Possibly not.'

'She was after his money?' Jodie asked indignantly.

'Your father had a lot more than money to offer her,' he answered enigmatically. 'And he was crazy about her. As you can imagine, he became increasingly agitated when there was no reply from you.'

'But…why didn't he write to me again?' she wailed.

'I don't know. Perhaps because he wasn't at all well,' Morgan explained. 'He had a lot on his plate. He and his fiancée were moving house—to here—with all the usual upheavals that entails—choosing carpets, buying antique furniture, paintings, visiting the London silver galleries, re-building the kitchen, landscaping the gardens….'

'Good grief! No wonder he was ill! That would have taxed anyone his age!' she exclaimed in concern. 'He should have been taking it easy—'

'I know that,' Morgan said wearily. 'But he was indulgent and could refuse her nothing, particularly as he was keenly aware that his fiancée was afraid she'd end up as a mistress, rather than a wife. Constant delays to setting a wedding date caused endless friction. It wore Sam down and privately he blamed you. One day, he and his fiancée had a blazing row, and when he wouldn't respond to her ultimatum, she stormed out. She'd been drinking and her judgement was impaired by that and by anger...possibly fear, too, that she was being strung along. She drove into the path of an oncoming lorry and...' His voice broke. He bit his lip and turned away.

Jodie stared in horror. The robe stretched taut across his tensed back and she ached to console him. But she'd inadvertently caused the tragedy. She could do nothing. Her fluttering hands fell to her sides and never had she felt so useless in the face of someone's grief.

'Oh, Morgan!' she whispered sadly, and her own voice faltered. What could she say? Words were inadequate. A hug would have been the answer, but that was out of the question.

His head lifted a fraction. 'Your father was taken to hospital in shock. She died a short time later of her injuries,' he said, the low mutter betraying how deeply he'd been affected.

It was extraordinary that Morgan should have cared so much for this woman. But he had, perhaps because she'd brought happiness and love to his friend's life.

Whereas she... Jodie fought back the tears. Everything was horribly clear now. Morgan's utter hostility, her father's rejection of her.

'I'm so sorry. So terribly sorry. Poor woman...my poor father,' she said brokenly. 'No wonder he hates me. And you do, too.' She felt miserable, but at least she knew where she stood. 'Thank you for telling me,' she said, feeling drained. 'It puts me in the picture.'

And despite his antagonism she had to make a gesture, to show how she felt. Impulsively she went to his side, her heart wrenching at his ferocious frown. Tentatively she touched his arm and he started.

'You must have taken the brunt of this dreadful situation,' she observed gently. 'My father ill, his fiancée dead… You must have been the person he turned to, to unload all his grief. Presumably you handled the funeral—'

'Yes,' he agreed tersely. 'Sam couldn't attend.'

'And there would have been the house to organise, my father to visit, chores to be done…so much. You've been through a lot too, haven't you?'

He sawed in a long breath and shook his head slowly. 'I don't know what to make of you, Jodie!' he said in a low tone.

'I am what you see,' she said simply. 'I care very deeply about things. I'm not irresponsible or shallow. I wish I could convince you of my honesty. I swear to you on my father's life that I am *not* lying about sending several letters to him. I don't mind accepting responsibility for all kinds of things, but neglecting to reply to him isn't one of them. Those letters went astray—or were deliberately kept from my father.'

He raised a querying eyebrow. 'Why do you say that?'

'Because I *know* the letters were posted. That means those are the only two possible explanations,' she said quietly. 'I have to say that the woman here wasn't very helpful, and that's putting it mildly. On both occasions when I phoned and told her who I was she told me to take a running jump—'

'A…what?' he exclaimed, grabbing her wrist urgently.

Suddenly she knew there was a chink of light, a chance that he might know who this person was.

'A running jump!' she repeated, her eyes bright and searching. 'Was it the daily help? She sounded young. Very off-hand and dismissive, and she put the phone down on me when I got emotional. Oh, I thought she had a very faint Irish accent, if that helps.' She waited, scanning his face anxiously.

Irish! Morgan groaned and passed a hand over his face. Teresa had never been able to disguise her Dublin background, despite all her expensive elocution lessons. And the expression 'take a running jump' had been peculiar to Teresa. She'd used it often—whenever she lost her temper. That was how they'd lost two good daily helps.

Appalled, he gazed down at Jodie's upturned face and felt like grovelling. 'I think it's possible I've misjudged you,' he said huskily.

Her eyes widened to mossy pools of light and her lips parted as she said breathlessly, 'You know who it was, don't you?'

He felt his heart leap and buck, found himself drawn closer. The satin of her skin beneath his fingers throbbed deeply, and he didn't know whether that was from her pulses or his... He clung on hard to keep his sanity.

'Teresa,' he managed. Common sense told him to remove his hand. Instead, he let his fingers spread out over the fragile bones. She looked puzzled and he expanded. 'Sam's fiancée.'

'But...' Her eyes grew enormous. 'Why wouldn't she want me around?'

That mouth...the soft arch, the hopeful curl at each corner... Morgan slicked his tongue over his lips so he could answer without croaking like an idiot. But the little shudder that ran through her was almost his undoing. He'd taken a step closer before he realised and he had difficulty keeping his mind on his answer.

'Remember, she didn't know why you'd been contacted. Sam's friends...disapproved of Teresa. Perhaps she feared you would too, and might try to influence him adversely. Who knows? As I said, she was desperately eager to get married,' he added, omitting to say why—that she had already been carrying another man's child and time had been running out on her.

She bit her lip. 'It's tragic!' she said passionately. 'I suppose it was she who threw away my letters?'

'Very likely,' he said heavily.

Pain lanced through him. Teresa had caused mayhem. Sam's life, his, Jack's, and now this tender-hearted woman's future had suffered because of Teresa's insecurity and dogged determination to be the wife of a wealthy man.

'There's a terrible irony in this. Without realising it, she prevented her own marriage!' Jodie mused unhappily.

'If she'd known,' Morgan agreed, 'she would have welcomed you with open arms. And...'

He winced, thinking of the repercussions. Only because Teresa had known she was dying had he discovered he was a father. If she had married Sam he would have been in complete ignorance. But he'd held his son in his arms and had fallen hopelessly in love with him.

Because of Teresa, Jodie had been upset unnecessarily by what she'd imagined was Sam's rejection. Consequently Teresa had lost her chance of marriage and she'd brought on her own death. Because of that, Sam had succumbed to shock and then pneumonia, which must have shortened his life expectancy, and the future was a potential mess. He shook his head in disbelief at the cruel quirks of fate.

'If only she had let you come,' he said heavily. 'She would be here today.'

'It sounds as if you were very fond of her,' she said delicately.

He turned away, his shoulders high with the terrible agony of futile wishing. And then a little voice in his head told him that he had benefited by Teresa's death because he knew the joy of fatherhood. He couldn't deal with that.

'I don't want to talk about her,' he jerked out.

'No. I'm sorry. I didn't mean to intrude on your grief,' she said hastily, painfully sweet, heartbreakingly gentle and solicitous of his feelings.

A surge of sympathy for her threatened to overwhelm him. She'd had some tough things to face since arriving here.

'And your own grief?' he asked, facing her again.

She gave a brave smile and he felt more of a heel than ever.

'I feel keenly for my father's unhappiness and for his ill health. I dearly want to do what I can to help him,' she said earnestly. 'If that means walking away, then that's what I'll do. But I think I might have something to offer. He has you, but I'm his flesh and blood, all he has in the world now!'

He stared at her eager face, the love for a father she'd never known glowing in her soft eyes. She was one of those rare women—unselfish to a fault, caring and compassionate, and with a heart that longed to embrace the world. And he'd almost thrown her out!

Sam ought to know his daughter before he died. She deserved that much. And it would bring Sam happiness.

He shut out his own needs, determined now to do what was right. 'Jodie,' he said softly, 'when your father is a little better I will tell him what happened to the letters. We'll take it from there.'

'You mean about his fiancée keeping me away?' she said doubtfully. 'Wouldn't that upset him?'

He gave a rueful smile. 'Leave it to me. I'll make sure he understands why she took such precipitate action. I don't want to lie to him.'

'You're a very honourable man,' she sighed.

He wished that were true. 'I'm afraid he couldn't cope

with seeing you now, Jodie. Are you prepared to bide your time till I can talk to him and break it gently?'

'Anything!' she said fervently, her face wreathed in smiles and her eyes misting with happiness.

Somehow his hands had found their way to her shoulders, and he was frowning because he wanted to cup her face and kiss that tremulous mouth, whisper promises he might regret.

But her innocent, accepting face stared back at him with such joy and hope written there that he found himself saying, 'It might take a while. Why don't you stay here? Make yourself at home.'

She beamed in delight. 'Can I? That would be perfect. I'd be able to hear from you every day how he was, then. And I could help with the washing and keep the house clean—'

'But not cook!'

'Not if you want to live!' she said with a laugh.

He grinned back at her, worryingly elated that she would be here, under the same roof.

There was one problem still nagging at his mind: Jack. He needed time to decide how to handle that. He checked his watch. Jack would surely be waking now. And something still held him back from inviting Jodie up to see him.

'There's something I must do. Will you excuse me for a while?'

He grabbed a bottle from the fridge, concealing it from her, and hurried out before she could comment.

His own subterfuge puzzled him. She was everything Sam would wish for in a daughter: genuinely sweet and honest, courageous and thoughtful. Musing over his secrecy, he entered the nursery and bent over the cot, his love for Jack easing all the anxiety from his face and replacing it with a tender smile.

Whatever Jodie's character, she still remained a threat to Jack's future. OK, he corrected, a threat to the future he'd planned with Jack. Was he being selfish? What would be in Jack's best interests?

He reached down into the cradle and lightly touched the small closed fist. It opened and gripped his finger hard.

Jodie would love Jack, he thought helplessly. And she'd be a wonderful substitute mother to him—a million times better than Teresa, who'd planned on employing two nannies to 'cope with the kid'.

But he'd be a great father! He'd relearnt all the old nursery rhyme books already, studied child development, invested in some books on child health, explored the pros and cons of organic food, environmentally 'kind' nappies...

It was between him and Jodie, then: which of them was best fitted to care for his child? He leaned over and kissed his son's rosy cheek and he knew that his own feelings for Jack were too fierce for him ever to walk away.

Morgan sighed heavily. How the devil could he work for the reunion between Sam and Jodie—and at the same time end up in charge of Jack, who had been registered as Sam's son?

Biting his lip at the impossibility of the dilemma, he heard a sound and jerked his head around, his heart racing. Alarm lanced his eyes before he could control his reaction to seeing Jodie there, her face wreathed in soft smiles.

A sensation like a clap of thunder rolled through him. The decision had been taken out of his hands. She would adore her 'half-brother'. Would want to take him over *now*. Dear God, he thought in anguish. It had come sooner than he'd imagined.

'I didn't mean to disturb you,' she whispered. 'But I was passing and...oh, Morgan, can I come in to see your baby?'

'My...' He swallowed. Of course! She had no reason to think he might be Sam's! But he must tell her. 'I'm not—'

'Oh, please!' she breathed. 'I won't make a sound, I promise.'

He hesitated. What was it called...a lie by omission? Being economical with the truth? Yet this *was* his son. There was no deceit in that. He raised his head and met her pleading eyes.

'It's almost time for him to wake up,' he conceded, unwillingly touched by the radiance of her smile.

She tiptoed to the crib and crouched down, her face awed. 'I knew it was a boy because of the blue everywhere,' she whispered. 'What's his name?'

'Jack Samuel.'

She was too close to him. He could see each one of her long lashes as they fluttered above those amazingly clear green eyes. Her skin was flawless as a baby's itself, her expression too eager and her lips too inviting.

He sat the bottle in the warmer and tried to deal with the conflicting emotions roaring in his head. He wanted her to think his son was the most beautiful, most adorable baby she'd ever seen. And he also wanted her to find babies a total turn-off.

'He's just perfect!' she said shakily, and he detected the suspicion of a tear in the corner of her eye before she brought her hand up and rubbed there, impatiently. 'Oh, look! His lashes are fluttering—aren't they long and black? Like yours. And all that dark, wavy hair... Is he anything like his mother?' she asked with a laugh in his direction.

He frowned, his mouth pinched. 'I can't see likenesses,' he grated.

'I've said something wrong! Is—isn't she...around?' she asked tactfully.

Deceit... It soured everything he did: his love for his

son, his relationship with Sam and now Sam's daughter. But he couldn't bring himself to unburden himself to Jodie, or to say anything which would ultimately result in the surrender of his son.

Jack would be his. Always. His baby's face was imprinted on him like a video screen constantly before his eyes. The little squirming body was as familiar to him as his own. They were one and the same, indivisible.

'No,' he muttered. 'She's not around.'

Her hand enclosed his and when he met her sympathetic eyes he felt like groaning in frustrated anger and telling her that he did not deserve her compassion. She would not look on him so trustingly if she realised what he was hiding from her.

'He's waking!' she cried in delight as Jack uttered a little squawk. 'Oh, his eyes! Black as ink! I thought all babies were blue-eyed?'

'Jack's are. Midnight-blue,' he managed, knowing every shade of those huge bright eyes. 'Indigo-denim in bright sunlight. They look black in the semi-dark.'

He lifted his son out. 'Hello, there,' he said softly, holding him close to his face. His hand cradled the back of the small, warm head. He could feel the curls, flattened by sleep and body-heat to the back of Jack's scalp. 'Look at the sunrise,' he murmured, turning the baby around to see the rays of gold and amber pooling on the nursery floor. 'We'll go out later. We can listen to the birds, see the sheep and hear them bleating...'

He remembered Jodie and glanced at her. His gaze faltered, shaken by the intensity of her emerald eyes.

'I...talk to him,' he said, explaining himself and laying Jack on the changing mat.

A pain was racking her. It was sweet and hurting at the same time. Morgan had lost his wife—or she'd left him—

and he was devastated. The hurt in his eyes had been so strong when she'd mentioned the baby's mother that it was as if he'd been ripped apart.

What a lot he'd had to suffer, she thought sadly, watching his deft fingers undoing the pearly buttons on Jack's sleepsuit.

She quivered, unbearably touched by his tenderness and the deep love he had for his child. His hands seemed huge, but he manipulated the baby with a sure confidence which suggested he'd been doing this for some time. How long? she wondered.

'How old is he?' she asked longingly, wishing with all her heart that she had a good man in her life and the prospect of a baby of her own.

'Five weeks. He's putting on weight like a Sumo wrestler,' Morgan said, pride in every line of his face. 'And he recognises me. He always calms down if he's crying and I speak to him—or even if I sing. Poor child's clearly tone-deaf.'

She was enchanted by the picture he'd presented. She sat back on her heels and watched the cleansing and changing and hoped he'd ask if she wanted to hold the baby. But he didn't.

So she contented herself with enjoying the sight of Morgan, sitting in a chair and feeding his son, a quiet air of contentment pervading the whole nursery.

'This is a side of you I couldn't have imagined from our first meeting,' she said wryly.

'We are all complex people, Jodie. Multi-faceted, hard, soft, kind, ruthless, depending on the circumstances or the threat to our continued existence.'

'And you were prepared to growl like a bear and yell at any flibbertigibbet who threatened my father's well-being,' she said with a grin.

'I'd defend the people I love with every last breath in my body,' he replied.

'You're very loyal.'

'I love very deeply.'

An older man, a tiny child. The strong caring for the weak. She smiled warmly and was delighted when he smiled back.

'You can be very intimidating! I like you best like this,' she said.

He laughed. 'Me too!' He crossed his long bare legs at the ankles and gazed fondly down at his son.

Jodie's heart lurched and she recognised that she was dangerously on the brink of finding Morgan too appealing for her own good. Looking around, she found something to defuse her sentimental yearning.

'He's a lucky little boy,' she mused, admiring the cheerful trees which had been painted on the walls, with their huge eyes and smiling mouths. 'This is a wonderful nursery!'

Morgan looked pleased. 'I did it,' he said in an off-hand manner which didn't deceive her at all.

'You?' she cried, in amazement. 'But you're a brilliant artist! I especially like the fat robins. And that's the fairy castle of any child's dreams.'

'I enjoyed doing it. Didn't take long,' he mused.

She turned around, seeing that the bright, primary colours of the landscape had been continued across a bank of cupboards, and a bookcase had been disguised as a mountain.

'Are you a professional artist?' she wondered.

'In a way. An architect, like your father,' he replied.

She gave a surprised gasp. 'Morgan, that's what I wanted to be!'

'There's nothing to stop you, if that's what you want to do,' he pointed out.

'No, there isn't!' she cried, her face aglow with the sudden realisation. 'It's been my ambition ever since my teacher said I had talent in that direction.'

'So what did stop you?' he enquired.

'My foster-parents. They needed me to leave school and go to work so I learnt to type instead.'

'How did you feel about that?'

'Sad,' she acknowledged. 'But they were short of money. I felt it was right that I should contribute to the family income.' She smiled. 'I was always drawing as a kiddie. I longed to create something that I could walk past every day of my life,' she said passionately. 'It must be a wonderful feeling to know that a building is your concept, your idea turned into reality.'

He laughed. 'You sound just like your father!' he said in amusement. 'That's how he inspired me. And you're right. It's one hell of a buzz to see your dream, to walk around it and into it, to see it working on a practical scale and filled with people.'

Envious, she brought her knees up to her chin. 'Tell me more about my father and his work,' she begged.

'How about a description of him first?' Morgan lifted an expressive eyebrow and smiled when she nodded eagerly. 'OK. He's sixty, with all his own teeth and a good deal of thick white hair which flops on his forehead and he keeps sweeping back impatiently.' He grinned fondly. 'When he's working it often ends up streaked with the colours he's used.'

Jodie laughed with him at the picture he was painting. 'I can almost see him,' she said softly. 'Is he tall, short?'

Morgan's voice grew quieter than before. 'Tall. He used to have a powerful build but now he's thin and drawn, all cheekbones and jaw. He has your eyes. Less bright, not as clear, but still with the ability to sparkle when he's excited about something. I suppose...I suppose he has a similar character to you.'

'What's that?' she asked warily.

'Honest, good, kind, generous...' He stopped the surprising list of attributes and let his mouth curl wickedly. 'Stubborn, passionate, single-minded and occasionally impossible!' he added.

She giggled. 'There could be fireworks if he and I ever disagree! But...I'm glad to hear he's a good man. Mom never said anything about him, but when I grew older I put two and two together. Knowing what I did of Mom, I assumed that he told her to leave because she was having an affair.'

'I believe that might be true,' he said with great tact. He lifted Jack up a little once or twice and was rewarded with a small belch and a dribble of milk. Jodie then realised why his jumper had been slightly stained at their first meeting. 'Good boy!' he said approvingly, as if, she thought with a smile, the baby had successfully mastered algebra.

'You dote on that baby!' she teased.

He shot her a sharp look from under his brows. 'Yes,' he said, looking defensive.

'Calm down! I approve,' she giggled.

He gave a thin smile. 'I get a bit protective,' he explained a little sheepishly, and hastily changed the subject. 'We were talking about you, though. You said your mother died when you were six?'

'That's right—eighteen years ago. I've wanted to belong to someone ever since,' she confided. She leant forward, once more hoping he'd ask her to hold the baby. Instead, he stood up with Jack tucked in one arm, dealing efficiently with the debris around him. 'Can I help?' she asked.

'No.' He amended that rather curt refusal. 'Thanks. Tell me about your foster-parents.'

Diverted, she made a face. 'They were tough on me. Sometimes I wondered if they only wanted the money I brought into the house. I can't remember either of them ever playing with me or cuddling me. Still,' she said cheerfully, 'they did give me a home, and I learnt to be self-sufficient and how to do chores.'

'But not to cook?' he asked drily, putting a cute little hat on Jack's head.

Jodie jumped to her feet and pre-empted Morgan, handing him the warm jacket he'd set his eyes on. But he wouldn't let her help to put it on the baby.

'My foster-mother taught me basic cooking. I always did our supper when I came in from school. When I left home, fancy cooking was beyond me because I was always scared of ruining expensive ingredients.' She grinned. 'I set the kitchen alight when I was doing a special meal for my boyfriend because I was so desperately anxious to please him. From then my nerves were so bad I seemed hell-bent on cremating everything, including lettuce!'

Morgan laughed long and loud, disconcerting Jodie utterly. The frown had been obliterated and replaced by appealing laughter lines, and the sparkle in his eyes and the dazzling whiteness of his teeth made her chest tighten up as if it were in a vice.

'I'm going to throw on some clothes and then we're going out for a blast of fresh air,' he announced. 'A walk along the footpaths and across the fields. Do you want to come?'

'Oh, yes,' she said happily. 'I'll fetch a jacket from my case.'

'Nothing else you need?' he murmured.

'Maybe a scarf. Why?'

'Sturdy shoes might be an idea, too,' he said drily.

She looked down at her bare feet, her face pink at her forgetfulness. She was too eager. She must throttle back or he'd think she was making a play for him.

'Shoes! Huh! You are so *conventional*!' she said in mock scorn, and ran quickly to her room before he changed his mind, his warm chuckle echoing down the corridor and making her skin tingle.

A little while later she heard him making his way downstairs and whistling up the dog, who had been sitting with resigned patience at the bottom of the stairs waiting for Morgan to reappear.

And she thought fondly of a time when they'd all be living here together: she and her father, Morgan and his baby. She knew that day would come about. Because she wanted it to, so very much.

CHAPTER SIX

THE air was fresh and sharp when they walked down the drive. Morgan had shrugged on a Barbour over jeans and a navy sweatshirt and tucked Jack into a baby pouch, which he'd slung across his chest. He chatted to his son with a natural ease that Jodie admired and envied. Loping by his heels, shadowing his every move, was Satan, totally devoid of a lead or any other restraint.

'Is he all right out here?' she asked doubtfully, when they came to the lane.

'Fine. He's intelligent enough to know that he must stay close to me, in case of a stray car. I'll let him run free when we're in the fields.'

'Unnervingly obedient,' she commented.

He must have noticed—and correctly interpreted—her askance look, because he smiled and said, 'Nothing to do with me. He's not my dog. Sam trained him. He and Sam went to classes and Sam learnt how to be consistent and clear, and not muddle his dog with confusing messages, and Satan responded with his utter devotion.'

Absorbing this, she happily breathed in the wonderful smell of the early morning—damp earth, the faint hint of pine—and thought how glad she was that Morgan wasn't a tyrant.

'And Satan accepted you, it would seem.'

Morgan rubbed the dog's head affectionately. 'Poor old chap. He couldn't understand it when Sam went into hospital. I had to spend some time getting him to trust me. We went for a lot of walks and I hurled a lot of balls before he did.'

More pressures, she thought. Sam, Teresa, Jack...the loss of his wife, coping with a bewildered dog—and now a long-lost daughter turning up.

It pleased her that she could stay and help. Keeping house would be a joy. And perhaps she'd get up the courage to cook something simple and get her confidence back. She beamed, feeling content for the first time in years.

Apart from the liquid sound of birdsong it was silent in the deep-cut lane. Morgan told her that it was an ancient Neolithic trackway, once cobbled with flintstone from quarries on the Downs.

'The area was heavily forested then,' he explained. 'So the tracks to and from settlements ran along the tops of the ridges and only occasionally dropped lower to the wild, muddy parts—perhaps to cross a river. We go over this stile. Satan goes under it.'

He held out his hand to help her over and once she'd dropped to the other side he did not relinquish it. For a short way they walked through the wood, while Morgan pointed out the snowdrops and emerging shoots of daffodils to the totally unaware Jack, with an engaging lack of self-consciousness.

'Why do you talk to him when he doesn't understand what the devil you're talking about?' she asked in amusement.

'So he can learn my voice,' he said, gazing tenderly at his son. 'I don't want him ever to forget it.'

'He's not likely to,' she said softly, loving the velvety tones now he wasn't angry and tense.

'No. It will be part of him. And all his brain cells will be alert and receptive because of the stimulation he receives—sound, sight, touch, smell… I've read a lot about this, you see,' he said earnestly.

'I'm impressed. I know nothing about babies or children,' she said, her face wistful.

'Neither did I. It was something of a crash course.'

'Oh. Yes, of course. How awful.'

'Jack had needs. I had no choice.' Deftly he turned the conversation away from himself. 'You and your boyfriend didn't…uh…consider a family?'

'I'd only have a child if I was married,' she replied firmly. 'And he wasn't interested in marriage or children. But…I'd love to have babies…'

'You will,' he said abruptly. 'When you meet the man you want to spend the rest of your life with.'

Suddenly he fell silent and she was left to wonder. Morgan was so near to her idea of the perfect man that she couldn't imagine herself with anyone else. She tried to block such inappropriate thoughts from her mind but failed miserably.

And she knew with a heart-thumping sadness that Morgan might be pleasant to her but he didn't exactly find her a turn-on. She didn't know what had happened to his wife, but he probably still loved her—and it would take a long time before he got over her.

'I want you to close your eyes,' he said suddenly.

Jodie opened them wider. 'What?' she exclaimed.

'Trust me,' he said with a faint smile. 'Something I want you to see at its best. A surprise. Close them.'

Pretending to grumble, she did so, and his arm came around her waist to guide her along the path. They must look like lovers, she thought, her heart thumping hard.

Beneath her feet she felt the twigs, leaves and mud of the woodland suddenly change to springy turf. 'We're out of the wood,' she declared, when they came to a halt.

There was a long pause. 'Not entirely,' he replied, in a cryptic tone.

'Well, it feels different,' she demurred.

'Yes. It does feel different to what's gone before,' he agreed huskily. 'Wait. Keep your eyes closed.'

It was hard. He was breathing softly beside her, his hand warm and firm, his thigh against hers. The breeze whispered over her face, making her lips tingle. And as his hand moved away to her shoulder she let out an involuntary sigh of disappointment.

'Come forward a little,' he said, loath to release her, longing to watch her expressive face unobserved for a few more moments.

She stood there in her scorchingly bright yellow trousers, red boots and an orange jacket, which she'd teamed with a fuschia-pink scarf and gloves, and the whole ensemble made him want to smile in sheer delight at her outrageously determined cheerfulness.

Her childhood had been hard and almost loveless, and yet she'd emerged as a positive, outward-looking person. He admired her tenacity, her *joie de vivre*, the way her hair curled in little wisps around her forehead, how her cheeks glowed from the walk, the soft lusciousness of her lips...

Something bucked inside him. He thought it wise to let his hand drop. 'Right,' he said, with a stab at briskness. 'Open them.'

The dark brown lashes fluttered and lifted and her gaze was captured immediately by the huge figure outlined on the hill ahead.

'That is incredible!' she breathed. 'What is it? What's it doing up there—can we go up to see it?'

He was pleased at her reaction. He'd hoped she'd be impressed. 'It's the Long Man,' he answered. 'The Giant of Wilmington. We'll go up to see him another day. It's a long hike up and I need to get back in a short while. Here. Let me put my jacket down on the bank and we can admire him in comfort.'

'I'll help,' she said, seeing him struggling to keep Jack upright while attempting to wriggle out of the coat.

She removed his coat for him and they sat side by side on its tartan lining, with Jack sleeping in his arms in blissful peace, rocked by the rhythm of the walk. Her face was rapt as she waited for him to speak and he felt his throat closing up with desire.

It wasn't sexual, but something else. An elusive yearning, a warm contentment, a feeling that this was a companionship he could cherish for the rest of his life.

And that both elated and alarmed him. He had enough going on in his life already, enough of a commitment to Jack and Sam and to the business without adding one more. He had to feel that—when everything righted itself again— he could have personal freedom. He needed to be independent, not to be tied to someone.

And yet…

'I'm admiring,' she said, her white teeth gleaming as she gave a little teasing laugh. 'Do I get a commentary as well?'

'Sure.'

He looked up at the huge outline of a man on the slope of Windover Hill, originally carved out of the chalk some five thousand years earlier. As always, he felt a little shiver of awe and amazement go through him.

'He's the second tallest human figure in the world. Over two hundred feet tall—I forget how much more. Probably Neolithic. No one really knows the truth. But the staves he's holding probably represent a doorway—and it's said he's part of a harvest fertility cult. He represented the mid- summer sun god, who brought light, warmth and a full belly; a guardian who made the crops grow.' He gestured with his hand. 'Look. There are Long Barrows on the hill where the people were buried and a prehistoric trackway, the old route taken by travellers from those times to quite recently. Flint mines... A mortuary area for the funeral processions...' He smiled at her entranced face. 'It's a fascinating area. I can't wait to explore it thoroughly.'

'Nor can I! You've picked up a lot of information in the short time you've been here,' she commented. She leant forwards, her knees up to her chin, her expression thoughtful.

'Only because I grabbed a couple of books from Sam's bedside and read to him during the long hours I sat with him,' he replied absently.

'You've been unusually kind to my father,' she declared, turning to face him. The wind blew her hair across her face and the sun warmed the strands to a gleaming copper. 'Without you he might not have survived. You must have improved his chances considerably.' Pushing her hair back, she hesitated, and then reached out to cover his hand where it rested on his knee. 'I'll be forever grateful to you for not abandoning him,' she said quietly.

'I couldn't ever do that.'

Her hair had escaped again and he leaned closer, dangerously close, reclaiming his hand to smooth the shimmering hair on both sides of her head and to arrange it behind her small ears. The skin was warm and silky there, and the feel, the smell of her, was so sweet to him that he had to swallow hard to stop himself from kissing her.

Sexual obsession, he told himself sternly, is for teenagers with exploding testosterone. But a small inner voice protested that there was more to his obsession than raw hunger...

'There is a special bond between you and my father,' she observed, her eyes starry. 'What is it?'

Talk. He had to talk. That would ease the ache in his loins. And the unnerving ache in his heart. Plus the emptiness. The first of those he understood only too well. The latter he could put down to a lack of breakfast. He had no ideas on how to explain the other.

'I owe everything to Sam,' he said simply.

He looked away, out to the ancient hill, and wondered if men and women over the millenia had always experienced conflicting emotions which tormented their sleeping and waking hours.

'I knew it was something like that,' she murmured happily.

His bones strained with the effort of not holding her. Every muscle was ready, tensed and expectant, waiting for the moment when he drew her to him and put that ecstatic face against his. Denying his own body, Morgan breathed long and hard. Never had his arms seemed so empty, their purpose so wasted.

'My mother was his secretary,' he told her, determined to sound, act, *be* normal again. 'She was eighteen when she went for a job at his practice—and she was pregnant.'

'With you?' Jodie surmised.

Nodding, Morgan stroked Jack's squashed cheek with a delicate finger, imagining what it had been like for his mother, alone, in a strange country and unmarried.

'She'd come direct from Bogota, Colombia,' he explained. 'The father—my father—wouldn't marry her.'

'Then you never knew him? I'm sorry, Morgan. You must understand something of the emptiness that I felt, the sense of…of a hole in your life that needs filling.'

He gave a wry smile. 'I do. I wouldn't have asked you in if you hadn't unwittingly touched a raw nerve.'

'I'm glad I did—and that we had something in common. We'd never have known one another otherwise.'

Tension hung perilously in the air. 'No,' he husked.

The threads between them seemed to pull him inexorably towards her but he resisted. She gave a small shudder and drew in a breath through her teeth.

'Cold?' he enquired in concern, reaching out and rubbing her back and shoulders. 'Do you want to walk on?'

'No. I'm all right. Let's stay here for a moment. I want to know more about your mother and my father.'

He let his arm remain casually across her shoulders. Just a friendly gesture. To keep her warm.

'It wasn't a sexual relationship, if that's what's worrying you,' he murmured. 'They became the best of friends. He recognised his own loneliness in her, I think. She was well educated and they enjoyed the same things, the same sense of humour.'

Jodie didn't speak. She was watching Satan rolling on his back in the grass. Morgan continued, wanting to prolong this tantalising intimacy for as long as possible.

'It's odd, how one small thing…a look, an unguarded moment…can change the course of a person's life—'

'Oh, yes!' she said fervently.

He mused that Jodie had come and pleaded to see her father, using the only words which could move him. And so he'd let her in, and now…

Where was he? He frowned. Oh, yes. His mother… 'The interview with Sam didn't go well,' he began, his voice rich with the warmth of memories as he recalled the times he'd begged his mother to tell him the story again and again. 'She was tense and guilty about keeping her pregnancy a secret. Her typing test was a total disaster, though Sam was kind about it, recognising she was nervous. But she broke down in tears because she assumed she'd lost the job. Over coffee in a nearby café, he got the whole story out of her—'

'I assume he employed her on the spot?' broke in Jodie with a broad smile.

'What else would he do? It was typical of Sam,' he said fondly. 'Great benefactor to lame dogs, distressed women and all kinds of lost causes. He took an interest in me when I was born—stood as my godfather—and we became very close.'

She sighed. 'I suppose you replaced me. A kind of surrogate son.'

'Do you mind that?' he asked softly.

'No,' she replied. 'He needed someone to love. Everybody does. If it had to be anyone who took my place, I'm glad it was you.'

For a long moment she held his gaze, and then lowered her lashes. He felt honoured by her statement. Touching her cheek with the back of his hand, he met her molten green eyes anew and smiled.

'He would have been a good father to you,' he said gently. 'When my mother died I was eleven and already living with him because Mum had been seriously ill for some time. Sam consoled me, gave me time to grieve and encouraged me to talk about my mother.'

'He sounds a wonderful person,' she mused.

'The best,' he agreed huskily. 'It seemed natural that he should bring me up. I was sent to the best schools, given every chance and encouragement. I was fortunate—and I know it. I bless the day that Sam came into our lives.'

She was looking at him with such open delight that his heart turned over. His breath clogged his lungs as her face seemed to change, his fevered imagination believing that her mouth had intensified its poppy-red hue and had swollen, demanding his kiss.

Pure wishful thinking. Morgan gritted his teeth, refusing to break the trust she'd placed in him...and wary of the seething emotions filling his heart and mind.

'I'm...' She swallowed and averted her gaze, proving she'd been alarmed by his unwelcome interest. 'I'm really pleased that my father is kind,' she said.

'More than kind. Encouraging. Supportive. He's set standards I can only hope to attain.'

Like honesty, he thought. How badly he'd let Sam down!

'I can imagine you're the apple of his eye,' she murmured. 'He must have been thrilled when you said you wanted to train to be an architect.'

'I even have the career you've always wanted,' Morgan pointed out ruefully.

'I'm definitely going to study,' she said, her eyes shining. 'I'll get there one day.'

'Good. And now we must go,' he said with great reluctance. 'Barges to tote, bales to lift... Here.'

He rose and held out his hand, pulling her to her feet. For a glorious moment she toppled, and laughingly caught at his arms to steady herself. Her glowing, beautiful face swam into vision, the laughter twinkling in her warm eyes. And then she'd exclaimed over her clumsiness and was occupied with helping him into his coat.

Jodie felt deliriously happy. She knew she'd pay for it later, that she'd sober up and realise how crazy she was to let her feelings run away with her, but she wanted this little bit of pleasure to heat her through and through, to wipe away all the pain and misery of the past.

For a short time she could enjoy herself in Morgan's company. Abandoning the nagging little warning in the back of her mind, she began to sing, and he joined in as they strode across fields and stiles, then down a lane through an enchanting village of old flint and Tudor-beamed cottages, twelfth, thirteenth, fifteenth-century, according to Morgan. The houses huddled together in a higgledy-piggledy fashion, their walls leaning in all directions, their gardens sprinkled with the nodding heads of snow-drops and the darker spears of emerging daffodils.

Behind her a hesitant January sun threw its beams on the river, and they paused for a moment while Morgan explained to Jack how to identify ducks and drakes and swans.

'Idiot!' she teased, her eyes warm with affection.

'He needs to hear language! He's going to be a genius,' he informed her with mock hauteur.

'Doesn't take after you, then,' she said rudely.

He was quiet for a moment and began to walk on. 'I wonder who he'll resemble?' he said under his breath.

But his mood had changed. His pace quickened and Jodie had to half-run to keep up. Anxiously she took a quick glance at his face and noted that it was stormy. She'd done it again. Reminded him of his wife.

They continued in silence and misery fell around her like a blanket. That made her feel worse. Maybe his wife had died. It was natural that he should feel his wife's death keenly. But Jodie felt dreadful for resenting the fact that Morgan wanted to cling to the past. Shamed by her selfishness, she strove to cheer him up.

'Right. Check your insurance and make your will. I'm going to cook for you,' she announced as they entered the back lobby, divesting themselves of shoes and coats.

He laughed, and she heaved a sigh of relief. 'A huge breakfast-cum-lunch because we've been up for hours?' he suggested. 'Can you cope with the Aga?'

'What's an Aga?'

'The stove.'

She raised an eyebrow. 'Can it cope with me?'

His eyes twinkled. 'Let me get Jack sorted while you get the food out, then I'll direct you imperiously from a comfortable armchair.'

It was odd, she thought, laying bacon on a rack and sliding it into the roasting oven, that she'd resented domesticity when she'd been with Chas. Yet here she was, eagerly offering her services! It felt different, somehow, though she couldn't identify why.

And his pleasure and praise for the nourishing meal made her glow all over. 'The eggs are a bit crispy,' she pointed out, not wanting to duck her mistakes.

'I like them that way,' he declared, enthusiastically attacking a lamb chop. 'And...to be honest, I probably wouldn't have cared if you'd charred everything. It's a pleasure to be cooked for.'

Jodie smiled, mentally planning on whisking around the house to ensure it was spotless and then conjuring up a simple but sophisticated supper. With wine. Candles... And she'd be wearing something gorgeous and sexy which whispered every time she moved...

She checked herself. Fantasising was OK, providing it didn't try to become reality. She'd better stick to her demure red jersey dress, pasta and electric light.

After they'd chatted and washed up together Morgan left for the office, saying he'd call in on Sam on the way back. It touched her that he took Jack with him.

'No thanks,' he'd said, when she'd tentatively suggested she could babysit. 'He always comes everywhere with me.'

'I understand,' she'd said in secret relief.

Her knowledge of babies was almost nil. Perhaps she ought to get involved with Jack—if she could ever prise him away from Morgan!

Humming to herself, Jodie set to with dusters and polish and a Hoover, enjoying herself enormously.

The house was tastefully furnished but had a cosy, loved feeling, and her father had collected some beautiful antiques; old oak furniture, silver and oil paintings being his particular interest, it seemed.

With the downstairs completed, she started on the large bedroom at the top of the landing. Searching around for somewhere to plug in the Hoover, she noticed that there were a large number of framed photographs on the top of a chest in the far corner.

Most had been knocked over and lay flat, perhaps when a drawer had been opened sharply. One was propped up by the others and she could see that the subject was a woman.

Probably Teresa, thought Jodie. This must be her father's room. And then she saw Morgan's robe on the back of the door—and sticking out of the laundry basket was the sleeve of the stained jumper he'd been wearing.

Her heart thudded. Morgan's room. Therefore... She looked towards the photos. His late wife!

Compelled by curiosity, she crossed to the chest, her feet sinking into the thick cream carpet. With great care, she collected one of the framed photographs and took it to the mullioned window to examine more closely.

Her face fell. 'Oh, she's beautiful!' she said out loud.

Morgan's wife stared back at her with dancing, roguish eyes, her blonde hair enviably long and artlessly framing a perfectly shaped face. She wore an evening dress and it clung to her like a second skin, the deep, revealing cleavage adding to the provocative nature of her pose.

There was no doubt that this was a very sensual woman, with the kind of sophistication Jodie had always envied. She could imagine her with Morgan, teasing him with those seductive eyes, arousing his Latin passions...equalling them...

Feeling sick, Jodie numbly rubbed the duster over the

frame and replaced it with the others, standing them all up carefully as she dusted each one. There were nearly twenty in all. Most were of Morgan's wife alone, posing in bikinis, designer outfits and ballgowns.

One or two showed her with Morgan, several were with a man who Jodie realised could only be her father.

She paused to study the handsome, laughing man who clearly had felt great affection for Morgan's wife, and she decided she liked the look of her father very much.

But Jodie was crushed by the sheer number of photographs. This was like a shrine. It pointed to a deep, all-consuming love.

She felt sad. For Morgan, for his wife and Jack, and also for herself. Morgan was one ideal man who'd married his ideal woman and who wouldn't settle for anyone else, anyone less exotic or beautiful.

Jodie felt a pang of dismay. She'd never match up to Morgan's wife. She grimaced. Her hair was the wrong colour, she was a good size larger, and she just didn't have that wicked air of danger about her.

Moodily she finished cleaning the room. She couldn't stop herself from touching his robe and then burying her nose in its folds. It smelled of him and she inhaled greedily.

'Oh, God!' she groaned, pulling back sharply in shock. 'I'm falling in love with him!'

CHAPTER SEVEN

MORGAN felt his heart lift as he came nearer to home. And the reason worried him. He was far too happy with Jodie, surprisingly content to be in her company. He liked watching her mobile, joyous face. He liked the sound of her laugh, her eagerness to devour life and her total lack of pretence.

At work he'd been absent-minded, a fact unusual enough to have drawn comment and concern. Later, sitting by Sam's bedside, he'd actually found himself chafing to get away. And so he'd punished his lack of attention by staying longer, even though Sam had been so drugged—after a difficult night—that the older man had barely known anyone was there.

'You fool!' Morgan muttered to himself in astonishment as he turned eagerly into the lane. 'You're actually nervous!'

And so he was. His hands were shaking for absolutely no reason at all. Hastily he checked his appearance, frowning and smoothing down a stray lock of hair—and then uttered a short grunt of annoyance at his action.

When he reached halfway down the drive Satan ran up to the car, barking ecstatically. Morgan parked in front of the house and climbed out, giving Satan a hug and hushing him.

He heard the door open and deliberately kept his head down, his arms around the dog. But his pulses were beating a tattoo everywhere they happened to appear in his body.

'Morgan!' Jodie cried, her voice sounding shaky. 'Thank

heavens! I thought my father had taken a turn for the worse or...or...you'd had an accident!'

Then he looked up. She'd been crying. Her mouth looked crumpled, her eyes pink-rimmed. 'Jodie!' he cried, unfolding his body and surging towards her in sympathy. He checked his watch, groaned, and then his arms were around her before he knew what he was doing. 'I didn't realise—I'm terribly late! I'm sorry. I should have phoned—'

'No, you shouldn't!' she mumbled into his neck. 'I've no right to leap at you with nagging accusations. It's just that I was expecting you, and I waited, and you didn't come, and I hung around and kept going to the window, and you weren't there, and—'

'Hey!' he laughed, raising her face to his. 'You have every right.'

He kissed her forehead. Very good, he told himself. Brotherly. Unfortunately his loins had different ideas. An intoxicating fragrance had wafted into his nostrils and his hands were aching to explore the neat-fitting jersey dress which poured over her beautiful body like red-hot lava. Quickly he detached himself before she noticed his arousal.

'How's my father?' she asked breathily.

Morgan sobered up. 'He's improved a little, they tell me—though he was sedated and I didn't get much sense out of him.'

'As long as he's all right...' she mumbled. 'You'd tell me if they were worried about him, wouldn't you?' she asked, her eyes misty with emotion.

'I would,' he promised. 'Now. I'll get Jack sorted, pour us both a drink. Then I'll change into a sackcloth, roll in ashes, lie at your feet and beg your forgiveness for not phoning you.'

'Excessive,' she chided, all radiant smiles again, as he'd hoped, at his comically humble expression. She made a face. 'You can make yourself useful and fix the fuse box instead.'

It was then that he noticed the house was in darkness. 'Good grief! What happened? When?'

'When I turned on the lights somewhere around three-thirty' she replied. 'There was just enough daylight left for me to search for candles.'

Morgan carried Jack into the hall. 'I'll do the fuses after I've taken him up to the nursery. He should sleep through. Perhaps you'd grab that candelabra and light our way. Your boyfriend didn't teach you about fuses, then?' he enquired, probing.

'I met him when I was seventeen. Chas had strong ideas on what women should do and fuses were men's work,' she said drily.

'You...mentioned thongs,' he said, hating her boyfriend with a deep and abiding passion. She wasn't the thong type.

She shuddered. 'Vile. You don't want to know,' she mumbled.

He was pleased by her evident loathing. He glanced across at her, feasting on the soft glow bestowed on her by the candlelight. And was that a blush on her cheek? And a faint tremble to her mouth?

She'd been scared, alone in this big house. He felt overcome with regrets.

'I'm sorry,' he said abjectly, as they entered the nursery, 'that you've been in the dark all this time.'

She started. 'Do you mean in the dark as in the ex-boyfriend, or as in the light failure?' she asked warily.

'Whatever fits,' he said, hoping to encourage her to open up. He wanted to know everything about her. To listen to her describing her life, her hopes, ambitions...

'It was quite romantic, really,' she mused.

'Being with Chas?' He shot her a dark look from under his brows.

'No! Using candles here! I didn't mind at all, though cooking wasn't too easy. I did worry about what had happened to you and Jack. You'd said eight on the dot, you see, and—'

'I know. I'm an inconsiderate swine,' he said vehemently, divesting the sleeping Jack of his day clothes. 'I had so many things on my mind... Uh-oh. There's a nappy needs changing here.'

He had the dirty nappy half undone when the phone rang and he waited while Jodie answered it.

'For you. Gordon Cook,' she told him, covering the receiver.

'My secretary. Must be urgent. Can you carry on?' he asked.

She was half-appalled, half-delighted. In at the deep end, she thought, grabbing from him the ends he was holding. A *dirty* deep end, she reckoned, gingerly starting to clean the little pink bottom.

'What do I do now?' she hissed, helplessly holding baby wipes.

'Put those and the inner gauze in that carrier bag I put ready. They're for dumping. Wet liner in the nappy bucket for recycling,' he flung rapidly, before continuing with his call.

She managed that, and found some cream and fresh liners and gauzy strips in the changing bag. And then began the struggle. Try as she might, she couldn't work out how everything went together. And when she thought she was almost there, Jack stirred, kicked his legs, and dismantled her beautifully constructed arrangement.

Worse, Morgan was laughing. 'I've got to go,' he chuckled. 'Major disaster area here... No, only Jack needing me. See you next week. Cheers.'

Red-faced, she started again. 'Why don't you use disposables like the rest of the world?' she muttered crossly.

Chuckling, Morgan knelt beside her. 'Precisely for that reason. Environmental conscience. Let me.'

'No—I want to learn!' she protested, disappointed that she couldn't show him what a natural mother she was. 'I only need showing how. It's not rocket science, is it?'

'Like this. Take it round—no, that's too loose...' Gently he guided her fingers, then picked up a sleeping suit decorated with blue rabbits. 'See? Easy when you know how. He can have a bath in the morning. I'll put him to bed now. Pop the clean vest on, then the sleepsuit,' he requested.

'*That* vest?' she cried, aghast. 'With that minute opening? It'll never go over his head!'

'It will. Trust me,' Morgan murmured in amusement.

'Hmm. Well, if you say so. I'll give it a go. Oh, his head's so heavy!' she exclaimed, gingerly lifting it.

Her eyes were huge and terrified with the idea that she could easily harm this child with a clumsy movement. She had a missing motherhood gene, she thought moodily.

'Support his neck,' Morgan advised when the head wobbled in an alarming way. 'His muscles aren't very strong yet.'

The tiny skull lay in the palm of her hand. With the other hand she was supposed to wrestle that vest over the baby's head. It seemed an impossible task even for a rocket scientist, unless he had four hands in total.

Mesmerised, she stared at the beating pulse in the dip at the front of Jack's skull, suddenly horribly aware of the extreme fragility of the tiny baby. This was Morgan's pride and joy, more precious to him than anything in the world.

'I can't do it! You take over!' she cried, panic-stricken.

'But—'

'No! I don't want to! I can't!' she wailed. 'Look at my hands! They're not steady enough. I'll drop him, I know. Take hold of him, Morgan, *please!*' she begged frantically.

'Of course,' he soothed. 'There's no reason why you should do this.' Deftly Morgan dressed his son, his movements so sure and confident that it looked easy. 'Come on, sleepy, you and your rabbits need tucking up.'

He scooped Jack up with enviable confidence and placed him in the crib, securing the blankets around the sleeping child and watching him, a tender smile warming his entire face.

The appalled Jodie remained on the floor, her lower lip trembling annoyingly. She'd failed the test. The little body had seemed frighteningly vulnerable to her lack of expertise and her nerves had ruined her determination to learn.

Her chest tightened with misery. Suddenly it seemed of overwhelming importance that she should be able to look after his child. In the back of her mind she'd seen herself running the house, looking after her father and being a kind of...nanny...to Jack while Morgan went to work.

Just now she'd just proved how useless she'd be. And she dreaded to think how much worse her efforts would have been if Jack had been wide awake, yelling and wriggling.

Her mouth drooped at the corners. Everything had gone downhill since she'd seen that photo of Morgan's wife. Her confidence had begun to desert her. Had her assertiveness been an illusion, then? Was she heading back to dependency and anti-depressants?

She felt sick at the thought.

'Have you eaten?' Morgan asked in a conversational tone, as he selected Jack's clothes for the morning.

She felt sicker. 'I had a sandwich,' she mumbled.

'No humble pie for me to eat, then?'

She wouldn't be cheered up. 'I did a pasta for us with a herb and tomato sauce, but...it's gone rubbery. You could make car tyres out of it,' she said, her face mournful. 'And I burned it whilst trying to keep it hot,' she added honestly.

'Then we'd better start again,' he suggested. 'After all, it was my fault I wasn't back at the right time—and I imagine you don't know how to keep things warm in the Aga. I'll give you a lesson.'

She sniffed, finding it hard to cope with his easy-going response. It had been his fault, but irrationally she still felt disappointed in her efforts. She'd wanted to welcome him to a warm house, with delicious smells wafting towards him which would be mingling alluringly with her new and expensive perfume.

All her painstaking cleaning and cooking, her new dress and carefully made up face had been to no avail. He couldn't see how spotless everything was without electric light, he'd not even noticed how nice she looked, and her scent must have been overpowered by the stink of incinerated pasta!

Her lip trembled. Discovering she had no natural aptitude with babies was the last straw!

'What's upsetting you?' Morgan murmured.

'Nothing.'

Sulky as a stupid child, she jumped up and went out, forgetting the lack of light. When she snapped on the switch outside the door she was met with a resounding nothing in the way of illumination, but pride prevented her from going back and she made her way to the stairs by feel alone.

And failed. Wrapped up in her own misery, she crashed into something hard, doubled up and gave a loud yell of pain.

'Jodie!'

Both light and Morgan appeared in seconds and his arms came securely around her.

'I hit my shin!' she gasped. 'Stupid, *stupid*!'

'Don't cry,' he said gently.

'I'm *not*!' she cried, dashing her fists across her eyes. 'What would I cry for?' she demanded shakily. 'Just because I'm the most cack-handed woman in the world where babies are concerned, just because I totally f-forgot the electricity was off and—and I was too pathetically silly to admit that and g-go back for a candle...'

'Slow down,' he murmured lazily, his blurred face swimming inches away. 'None of this matters. Remember, you've been through a hell of a lot. Take a deep breath... Jodie... *Jodie!* Don't look at me like that,' he muttered thickly.

'Like...what?' she mumbled, trying to focus.

He groaned like someone in despair. She heard the metal base of the candelabra being placed on a table, then felt the soft touch of his tongue on her upper lip, and before she could work out that he'd lapped up a salty tear his mouth was driving into hers, hard, firm, determined and totally abandoned.

'I'm sorry. I must!' he whispered into her hot mouth.

Something terrifying leapt within her, a wild, frantic hunger that fought for freedom, snapping the overstretched thread of restraint and flinging her headlong into a dark, unknown world of flames and heat which licked through her hungry body and turned it into a smouldering furnace.

'Yes!' she moaned.

Her hands reached up fiercely to rake his hair, feeling the silk between her fingers, the warmth of his scalp, as her mouth responded to his dizzying kisses with a ferocity that stunned her.

'God, you're beautiful!' he growled.

'Me?'

'Oh, yes, *yes*!'

She was all force, all need, all desperation. And he was, too, his groans echoing hers, his hands everywhere, like hers, every part of her demanding the relief as his questing fingers cupped, held, kneaded...

Her head rolled back and his mouth descended hotly on her throat, his lips finding the hollow where her pulse beat violently and moistening it with such a delicate sweep of his tongue that she moaned and whimpered as the sweet pain shot through her needy body, contracting her loins and rendering her totally helpless.

'Morgan!' she said on a sigh, and made an inarticulate, incoherent cry of longing when his teeth grazed her lower lip and his tongue tasted its swollen softness.

'Oh, yes!' he rasped.

His deep, shuddering tone made her go limp in his arms and she felt herself being borne backwards by the weight of his body... A welcome pressure, she thought with a groan of pleasure, the full force of his powerful chest and thighs moving her inexorably back and her own weak legs barely able to hold her upright.

And then they both collapsed onto the softness of a bed and she could forget the effort to stay on her feet and give her whole concentration to the wonderful sensation of being pinned helplessly by hot flesh and blood, hard bone and muscle...

Instinctively she arched against him, murmuring her hazy delight when her pelvis slid against his and encountered the hard shaft leaping from his loins.

Her legs wrapped around his body, reckless heels driving into his back and grinding him into her thighs.

'Please!' she whispered, beyond all modesty, all caution or rational thought.

It was as if something snapped in him too. His lips burned intense kisses on every inch of her mouth; his hands cradled her face with a vehemence that exhilarated her.

He shook with desperation and uttered a low, guttural cry, then sat back, the silvery moonlight in the room revealing his eyes to be hot with arousal as he frantically tore off his sweater, swooping down to kiss her senseless and then struggling to undo the buttons of his shirt with hopelessly incapable fingers.

She couldn't wait. She wanted him naked against her. In a quick movement borne of intense need, she sat up and dragged her dress over her head, then put her hands on the front edges of his shirt, ripping them apart.

And she buried her face in his chest, smelling him, kissing, nibbling and tasting. He jerked and gripped her shoulders when her mouth enclosed one taut nipple and, trembling with passion, he pushed her away.

'Too much,' he croaked in torment, catching his breath at the sight of her breasts, swelling luxuriantly above her scarlet silk bra.

'It isn't,' she husked desperately. 'It's not enough—'

Panting, she recognised the sexual greed in his dark eyes and a shiver of anticipated ecstasy rippled through her entire nervous system, intensifying the molten heat between her thighs.

'Touch me,' she whispered, her hands lifting her breasts for his delight.

'My God, Jodie—you...you are...perfect!' His growl was hoarse and thick with desire and she felt her nipples stiffening even more than before, thrusting painfully at the tightly stretched fabric.

One trembling male hand reached out. She watched, hypnotised with expectancy, her eyes drugged and limpid, her breathing harsh and moaning as his finger extended.

There was the briefest of touches through the silk, a faint slide across the taut swelling at the centre of her breast, and she bucked as if he'd sliced her through with a knife.

'Ohhhh!' she groaned. 'Again... So good... Touch me, touch me, Morgan!' she implored.

A thumb this time. She recognised its breadth, its greater heat. She swallowed, almost incapable of bearing the pleasure. Her head rolled back, her lashes fluttered in a plea that he should ease the agony of her other untouched breast.

Gently he slid the straps from her shoulders, his eyes burning into hers, holding her captive. He was too slow, too gentle...the tantalising drift of his fingers on her arms far too delicate. She wanted more. Now.

Her back straightened and the twin globes lifted free. The silk slithered down to her waist and she sat there, waiting, waiting, while he held his breath and the muscles in his chest snatched tightly into spasm then held rigid.

He devoured her with his eyes. His lashes lowered, thick and black against the gleam of his cheeks, and he drew in a short, hard breath that shuddered through him like a wave.

Slowly he shrugged his shoulders out of the shirt. She sighed softly and leaned back in a sinuous movement, raising her arms above her head. Moonlight turned his skin to polished silver, his Latin cheekbones sharply pronounced beneath his liquid tar eyes.

Intent on her, promising everything she longed for, he lifted a muscled arm and flung the shirt behind him. It hit something. Into Jodie's subconscious came the sound of an object slithering and then a crash followed by shattering glass.

Morgan's head jerked around. And he froze.

Jodie could see nothing. When he turned back she saw that a terrible anguish wrecked the beauty of his face, twisting his mouth into an agonised groan. Jodie sensed him retreating into some dark hell of his own, a place which had no corner for her.

Frantic to keep him, she pressed her aching body against his, the rigid peaks of her breasts scraping firmly, insistently, across his straining torso. Her arms twined around his neck and she kissed his tortured mouth.

'Morgan,' she whispered gently, seductively.

But his lips clamped together and she felt his jaw clench hard in denial. Firm hands clasped her arms, pushing her back. Bewildered and angry, she blinked up muzzily at his grim face.

'I can't!' he grated. 'Forgive me. I should never...'

He'd left the bed. Was picking up his shirt, jumper...shoes he'd somehow discarded...

'You can't...*go* like this!' she gasped jerkily, raising herself on her elbows.

He stopped, his back to her. 'I must!' he insisted.

'But...why? You wanted me!' she accused, deeply hurt. And unable to pacify her screaming, demanding body. She'd been so sure of him. And now she felt confused. 'What were you doing, Morgan?' she demanded miserably.

He remained silent, his shoulders in that now familiar rigid hunch. She slid her feet to the floor, intending to get some kind of explanation. And then she found one.

The shirt must have caught one of his wife's photographs which she'd arranged so carefully for him on the chest of drawers. It now lay face down on the floor, the glass smashed to smithereens.

Her stomach sucked in with nausea. Now she understood. He'd been desperate for sex. But smashing his late wife's photo had shamed him. He felt as if he'd betrayed his wife's memory.

Jodie curled up on the bed, her eyes huge as she quietly

drew the covers over her near-naked body. Competition she could cope with. But not a dead woman.

'If you'd keep your back turned for a while,' she said, managing a reasonably normal voice, 'I'll get dressed and you can have your bed back.'

Morgan bit back an urge to tell her why he couldn't make love to her. It had been a mistake to bundle the photos of Teresa on top of the chest. But Sam had said he couldn't bear looking at her and being reminded of her: alive, beautiful, glowing with health.

Morgan had hoped that one day Sam would take them back, for Jack's sake. Jack had a right to see what his own mother had looked like. They must not be lost or thrown away.

But when he'd turned moments ago and found Teresa staring at him with her wicked eyes he'd been reminded of his deceit. And something had clawed at his gut. Pounding relentlessly into his head had come the realisation that he couldn't make love to the open and trusting Jodie under false pretences.

Either he had to tell her the whole truth of the situation or he had to leave her alone. Any kind of relationship based on a pack of lies and half-truths was doomed to fail.

His breath caught in his throat. Astonishingly, he felt that he wanted to build a lasting relationship with a woman he'd barely met, hardly knew. And yet in a strange sense it seemed as if he'd known her all his life.

His hands stilled. *But what of Jack?*

He let the pain scythe through him in punishment for losing sight of his most passionate hope for his son's future.

Jodie—sweet, sexy, all woman—had turned his head. He dared not allow her to get too close. It was one hell of a risk. What if the relationship failed? She'd remain here with Jack, her 'half-brother'. And he'd have no rights to see his son ever again. She'd marry some other guy whom Jack would learn to call Daddy...

God! Why did he want two people who were totally incompatible with his peace of mind?

'I'm dressed now,' she said, behind him.

Numb with anger at himself, he pushed his arms into his shirt. 'I regret what happened—' he began stiffly.

'I understand.'

He whirled, his eyes intensely black. 'No! You don't—'

'Give me some credit!' she flared. 'I know what happens when a man is virile and red-blooded. I'm not some ignorant virgin. I'm familiar enough with the male urges to realise that you needed sex and I was around and willing.'

Touchingly, she lifted her head, as if she had no shame in that self-revealing statement. But it hadn't been the way she'd described: a purely animal desire to satisfy a rampant sex drive. It had been something different, something more profound. Though caution prevented him from saying so.

'But it's too soon, isn't it?' she went on, her voice jerking oddly. 'You can't bring yourself to betray your late wife...because you still l-love her.'

'What?' he muttered, puzzled.

Jodie's eyes looked sad. 'Your wife. I saw you looking at the photos,' she explained. 'She was lovely, Morgan. The kind of woman you—you'd never forget,' she finished, stumbling slightly over her words.

It sliced his heart in two to have Teresa referred to as his wife. As for never forgetting...that was true at least. He'd remember Teresa to his dying day.

'We need to talk,' he said, his mouth tight. 'Come downstairs. I'll fix the fuses and we'll eat some supper. There are some things you need to know.'

But how much should he tell her? He wrestled with his conscience that insisted everything. He couldn't go that far.

They went down the stairs in silence, avoiding contact, avoiding each other's eyes. Which was ridiculous when they'd been so close a few moments before. He could still smell the faint fragrance of her skin, feel the firm pressure of her body...

His teeth clenched together as desire rocketed through him. In one stupid moment he'd let down his guard and succumbed to his hunger for her.

He shuddered at his precipitate action. He'd been totally unprepared. Supposing he'd made love to her? Supposing she'd become pregnant? What the hell would he have done then? How would he ever have lived with himself? God, he was a fool!

Jack needed him. Jack would need his support and presence right through his life. How could he have put his son's future in jeopardy?

The easiest thing would be to ensure she didn't stay long. When the opportunity arose, he must, *must* tell Jodie what it would mean if she was reunited with her father. The future for Sam was very bleak, and maybe, like Teresa, she'd hate the prospect of looking after a desperately sick man.

Then the problem would be resolved. He could keep her at arm's length and then she'd leave and he and Jack would continue with their lives in peace.

But... He scowled. He didn't want Jodie to go! Why, he had no idea; he knew only that she occupied his mind and body with every breath he took.

Wasn't there a compromise somewhere? When he dwelt on the possibility of never seeing her again, the anger and resentment surged up within him, blocking out everything else. Dear heaven, what was happening to him?

His hands shook as he dealt with the fuse box. The lights snapped on, illuminating the house, all its surfaces sparkling where Jodie had obviously wielded a duster with spectacular results.

He didn't look at her when he walked into the kitchen. Instead, he selected a pizza from the freezer and popped it into the roasting oven, then started preparing a salad. She watched him from where she sat at the kitchen table, quietly waiting for him to speak.

Placing the salad and a dressing on the table, he pulled out a chair and sat down heavily.

'First, I want you to know that I have never been married, Jodie,' he said, his voice tight and strained.

She frowned, staring at him with her startled green eyes. 'But...the woman in the photos—'

'Is Teresa. Sam's fiancée.'

She sat back, stunned into silence. He could see her mind working on something which clearly puzzled her. And then she spoke, timidly, jerkily. 'You have loads of framed snapshots of her...I thought she *must* be your—'

'*No!*' It came out as a tortured denial, but that was how he felt.

'Then...why are they in your room?'

Cold inside, he leant his forearms on the table and stared down at the grain of the table, thinking ahead to the moment when he'd have to persuade her to go home. His breath raked painfully in his chest.

'Your father wanted them thrown away,' he said huskily.

'But...he loved her!'

'Yes. That's exactly why—because he...loved her,' he said, forcing out the words against his will. 'When your father heard the news of Teresa's death he went berserk, flinging the photos around like a man demented. He couldn't bear to see her; it was too painful for him. Then he collapsed and I took him to hospital.'

He stirred in his chair, recalling the distaste with which

he'd collected the scattered frames and flung them on the barely used chest in his bedroom.

'So...why are *you* keeping the photos?' she cried tensely.

'For Sam and...' He checked himself, realising he'd been close to involving Jack. Jodie would have demanded an explanation if he had. 'For Sam,' he amended, frantically trying to find a way to finish that sentence. 'And,' he said, relief flooding his face when the answer came, 'my reason was that I knew he'd want them again one day.'

'I see.'

It was a good answer—and perfectly possible. But Jodie knew something wasn't quite right. He was evading her eyes. The story didn't quite match up with what she sensed—or that telling little mistake which he'd hastily corrected.

For Sam and...who? For himself? Had he wanted some of those photos depicting Teresa at her sultriest? Could they still be a kind of shrine—not to his wife—as she knew now—but to the glamorous, utterly desirable Teresa?

Jodie felt her stomach turn. That slip of the tongue had betrayed his real feelings. *For Sam and for me!* She bit her lip as the truth brutally made itself known, and her eyes paled to a silvery hue. Morgan had been wildly infatuated with the stunning and provocative Teresa!

Rooting back in her memory, she now remembered the occasions when there had been some reference to Teresa. Every single time he'd responded with barely concealed grief—and there was only one possible explanation for that. Obsession.

Cold shivers ran down her spine. The situation, if it were true, was appalling. What about the woman who'd mothered his child? Morgan had been in a relationship with Jack's mother—and yet at the very same time he'd coveted his boss's mistress!

Helpless to stop herself shaking, she struggled with her sickening aversion to Morgan's secret passion for her father's lover. It couldn't be true. It must not be. She had believed Morgan to be a man of honour—but where was honour, she thought sadly, where obsession was concerned? It hit you like a blow, wiping out all rational thought, compelling you to behave out of character. She knew that only too well.

She stiffened. Perhaps Morgan was using her now—as he'd used Jack's mother…as a substitute for what he really wanted: someone to ease his frustration for the unattainable Teresa. She winced, unable to bear the degrading humiliation.

'Morgan, there's something I want to say,' she said decisively, her heart lurching with misery. Warily his eyes flicked up then, and met hers in query. 'It's quite simple.'

Her tone hardened with bitterness that she could have been so deceived by a man's coaxing words, the look in his eyes, the tender passion of his touch.

She'd believed he'd felt something special too. But when he'd touched her and looked at her he'd probably been picturing *Teresa's* face, remembering *her* scent, the curves of *her* body—

'You don't know what you've just done!,' she cried angrily, any restraint snapping with those images. 'Oh, you might be hurt. You might be upset. But that doesn't mean you can use me for therapy!' she yelled.

'What the hell do you mean?' he barked, leaping to his feet and glaring down at her white face.

'I mean,' she ground out furiously, 'that I will *not* be used as a sex object ever again! Not by you or by any man!'

'Sex object? And what was I?' he raged. 'Have you miraculously fallen madly in love with me?' Breathing hot and hard, he leant over the table, intimidating her. 'Or did you feel a need to satisfy some ordinary, basic desires—the same ones you accuse me of feeling?' he hurled ruthlessly.

'That's unfair!' she cried, colouring up.

'No, it's not! You wanted me as much as I wanted you!' He drew himself erect, simmering with temper. And something else. A dark, bitter expression permeated his entire face. 'So, Jodie,' he said in a low and gravelly tone, 'it may surprise you, but I don't want to be a sex object either. I don't want a woman to use me as a stud because she misses rampant sex with her boyfriend—'

'It wasn't that!' she gasped.

Suddenly still, his eyes veiled, he studied her for a long time. 'What was it, then? An emotional crutch?'

She lowered her head. There was pride, or there was the truth; there was the counsel of silence…or an attack in the form of a question.

'Is that what it was for you?' she mumbled evasively.

'Come to your own conclusion,' he snapped.

'I think I have! You wanted me because you're grieving over Teresa's death. You needed sex and you needed human comfort, the feel of a woman in your arms,' she accused, her voice shaking with pain and resentment. 'Get a whore for the job!' she flared. 'And keep your hands off me in future!'

Morgan drew in a long, chest-filling breath. 'And if I can't?' he said softly.

'You dare come near me again—!' she began, close to hysterics.

'Stop this, Jodie!' he said curtly. 'We've reached an impasse. You obviously can't trust me.'

'No. I can't!'

'In that case there's only one solution. It's time you

moved out. We've just proved that being here together is asking for trouble.'

It was as if the wind had been taken out of her. 'L-leave?' she stumbled.

'It would be best,' he said harshly. 'Why make life hard? If you go, there's no problem. I don't have to control myself.' He shot her a thoughtful, assessing look, as if he had more to say. 'And later, when your father returns here, it would spare you the worst of his illness.'

Jodie stiffened. 'What do you mean?' she asked, puzzled.

His face a cold mask, he leant back against the Aga and folded his arms in an attitude which suggested indifference to her feelings.

'He will never be well again, Jodie. His suffering will increase. Can you take more of the hard, blunt truth?'

Somehow she held herself together. Her eyes were wide and haunted when finally she managed to swallow back the clogging lump in her throat and reply.

'It sounds as if I must,' she said in a small, frightened voice.

'I'll get you a brandy.'

He was gone for a few moments during which she sat there shaking like a leaf. She felt as if she'd been through a sawmill. All her nerves were torn and ragged, her stomach lurching around as waves of nausea hit her.

A brandy balloon was thrust into her trembling hand. 'Drink it.'

When she stared at the glass in her hand, he took it from her nerveless fingers and held it to her lips. 'Drink!' he commanded.

It was hot and fierce and seared rawly through to her stomach. But it did the trick.

Morgan fought to hang on to his objective. Jodie had to go. It was true: he'd been without sex and without a woman's sweetness for too long. He'd misinterpreted his feelings for Jodie and in a short time he would forget all about her.

But Jack would still be there, Jack would be his—if he could only stick to his decision to keep Jodie at a distance—and keep her ignorant of the raw truths which could ruin Jack's life.

But it was hard. He had to give a good performance in the next few minutes, depicting a man with sex on the brain and ice in his heart. That would drive her out.

And yet she was sitting there trembling, eyes great green pools in the ghostly pallor of her face, tragedy etched across her downturned mouth. He reined in all sympathy and harshly jerked out the unvarnished facts.

'Sam was in the Far East working on a project some years ago. They were spraying toxic chemicals nearby. Gradually he began to get headaches, lapses of memory, bouts of sickness and so on. Last summer he had a checkup and they discovered massive damage to the major organs of his body.'

Her hand flew to her mouth as a moan escaped. Like a child, she clenched her fist and bit on it to stop herself from crying out again.

Jack, Morgan kept thinking. I'm doing this for my son.

But it didn't help. He wanted her to think well of him, not to appear an unfeeling monster. He ached to take her in his arms and explain gently. Forgive me, he pleaded silently, turning his back to her. And he occupied his hands by making a coffee, crashing china about unmercifully.

'What...?' Her voice had been just a hoarse croak. He heard her swallow and he gritted his teeth, spooning instant coffee into a mug. 'What treatment is he having?' she asked.

'There is none.'

'Oh, God!'

Sugar, he thought. Three. Anything to stop him turning around and seeing the misery on her face.

'That's why he wrote to me,' she said jerkily.

'Yes. He wanted to see you—and of course he wanted to marry Teresa before he deteriorated further.'

'Tell me what will happen,' she whispered. 'And,' she cried in agitation, her voice rising, 'stop fiddling about with that biscuit tin and darn well face me!'

Perhaps he should. His punishment. He stirred his coffee and glanced across at her, his jaw tight with tension. Tears were swimming in her enormous eyes and her lip trembled.

'I love him too,' he shot tersely.

'Yes. I know.' She bit her lip. 'Tell me.'

'Over a period of time he will become progressively confused, with fewer and fewer lucid moments. His lungs will give out and his heart will be put under excessive stress. He'll be forgetful and difficult, like someone with Alzheimer's. And...I'm told he'll lose control of all his functions.'

She said nothing and it seemed she was in shock. Unable to remain still, he restlessly quartered the room as he spoke in staccato sentences.

'We must do what's best for him. During his last conscious moments I want him to be happy. No stress. I will be plain, Jodie. I find you sexually desirable. But I need to concentrate on Jack, and on Sam.'

'Yes, of course,' she muttered.

'You may decide that you still want to be reunited with your father,' he went on. 'On the other hand, you might not. It would be a short-lived relationship which would give you great pain, and I for one wouldn't blame you for walking away. However, if you do decide to meet him, then I ask you to make things easier for me, for both of us.'

'How?' she whispered.

His strides quickened. 'Stay in a hotel, a flat—whatever you want. I'll pay for it. I just don't want you here. When he's well enough—after a spell in a convalescent home, perhaps—I will tell him about you and arrange for you to visit him here—'

'How long before you'd tell him?'

He shrugged. 'Two, three weeks.' He gripped the edge of a kitchen chair and whirled around, his face grim. 'And you must promise that when he no longer recognises you…'

He paused, overcome with emotion. That would be when he'd need her most.

'What?' she asked in a thin, reedy voice.

He controlled his selfish needs and glared at her ferociously. 'Then I want you to get out of our lives for ever!'

CHAPTER EIGHT

JODIE rose to her feet. And although her legs were shaking, she managed to remain steady by holding fiercely onto the edge of the table, her fingers white with strain.

'Unthinkable!' she snapped. 'Do you really expect me to pick and choose the kind of father I have? To only want a father who is in good health and able to respond to me?'

Morgan seemed disconcerted, his frown bringing his dark brows hard together. 'Just visit him, Jodie. See him when he's awake and settled—'

'*This is my father!* Why should I be sidelined when he needs me most—?'

'Because it will be hell looking after him!' Morgan rasped. 'Because I'm offering you a chance to hold a better memory of him in your mind—'

'Do you think I'm so shallow that I can't see beyond the shell of a person and into the heart and mind and soul? I know what my father's character is—you've told me. I will respect and love him whatever he looks like, however ill he becomes—'

'You can't take on his care,' he insisted grimly. 'And I won't have some ultra-efficient nurse bullying him—'

'Neither will I!' she retorted, horrified that he could even think of that. 'Maybe someone to help with the chores, to do the washing—but not to care for him. That's for the people who love him, who don't flinch at the unpleasantness and the sadness of seeing a loved one slowly declining—'

125

'You can't put yourself through that, Jodie!' he cried passionately.

'Why not?' she yelled. 'You are!'

'I'm different—'

'No, you're not! Oh, granted, I don't even know him. He's been your substitute father for most of your life, your friend, and the man you admire. But I have a deep and abiding need to know and love and cherish my father—and you can't take that from me!'

Too fraught to know what she was doing, she went to Morgan, catching his wrists in an urgent grip. He had to understand how she felt. She must win him over.

'You forget,' she cried, 'I've been a regular visitor to an old people's home in New York. I've seen things that would make your hair curl. I've watched men and women die and I hope I've made their last few moments easier by my presence, by holding their hands and talking to them till their spirits departed. Yes, it sears the emotions. Yes, it hurts. Yes, I cry when someone I've known has gone. But that's the reality of life and death and love and sorrow, and to know one you must at some time endure the others!'

'Jodie—!' he started hoarsely, his eyes glistening, dark and fevered.

'No, let me finish!' she insisted fervently. 'I don't shrink from what I have to do. It won't be easy. But this is my father we're talking about, and you can't deny me the right to make his life as comfortable as possible! I want his love. I want to love him, Morgan! You, with no father, must feel some pity for me! I have to stay in the house. I will need to be near him. We can work out a rota. You have Jack to think of. Let us share the care between us. *Please!*'

'Hell.'

He wrenched free of her grip and put a hand to his forehead, concealing his eyes. Abruptly he turned away. But she had seen the anguish that racked him and she knew she had hit raw nerves.

'Morgan,' she implored gently. 'Whatever our needs, we have to ignore them for my father's sake. We can do this. More than anything, I'd like my father to be fit and well, but he isn't, so that's what I must accept.'

'You have surprised me,' he said softly.

She blinked. 'Why?'

He came to her, close enough for her to feel the heat of his body. And he seemed less tense than before, his anger abated. She hoped she'd persuaded him. It was so important to her that she stayed, not only for her father's sake but because she wanted to help Morgan break the barriers he'd erected when Teresa had died. He needed to be free so he could meet someone, fall in love...

She frowned, hating that thought, jealousy slicing sharply through her body. And found Morgan's finger smoothing out the furrows on her brow.

'I am impressed by your passion and your devotion,' he said, his deep voice soft and low. 'Not many women would choose such a hard and thankless path. Think carefully about this. You could be surrendering a year of your life in exchange for increasing heartbreak.'

'I would do it for the *rest* of my life if needed!' she cried with all the fervent conviction of her heart.

'I do believe you would.'

Her eyes widened. She found that they were leaning closer to one another, their gazes locked, lips parted. And Morgan was swallowing, as she was, perhaps because he too was overcome with deep emotion.

Her heart clamoured in her breast. Unless she was mistaken, there was more in his eyes than a hunger for sex or comfort. He admired her. Respected her. A wonderful warmth washed through her veins. She smiled shakily.

'Say you agree!' she begged.

His eyes were an irresistible liquid black, drawing her even nearer, the intensity of his gaze making her breath shorten in her throat.

'I must ask you to think about this a little longer. Our passions, our emotions are overstretched, and the situation will get worse. We could both do something we regret. I admit that I have a need to feel a woman's arms around me,' he said huskily. 'I'm warning you for your own good. I've been to hell and back, Jodie. Sometimes I feel I'm still on my way.'

'I know,' she said, longing to ease that hell.

He frowned. 'That's the trouble! You're so damn understanding and compassionate! Having you, a beautiful and achingly desirable woman, around is tempting fate. I can't expect you to spend your time here wondering if I'm going to grab you. I'm not made of stone—and you are…irresistible.'

She blinked. Irresistible! Achingly desirable! 'Am I, Morgan?' she asked, unwittingly alluring.

He licked his lips, the tip of his tongue leaving a glistening sheen on his carnal mouth, and all she could think of was taking his face between her palms and pressing her lips to his—thus forcing him to concentrate on *her* and not Teresa.

'Jodie!' he said sharply, making her jump. 'Nurse your father if you want, spend most of the day here, but don't sleep here. Do you hear that? You *have* to leave!'

She gave him a level glance. 'Why should I? To salve your conscience?'

Morgan winced. 'To prevent a disaster happening,' he bit back.

So, he thought that making love to her would be a disaster! Huh! He wouldn't think that if they did! He'd be overwhelmed, thrilled and besotted with her! she thought indignantly.

Hadn't he almost lost track of reality in her arms? If he hadn't broken that photo, wouldn't they now be snuggling up to one another, glowing and sated in the aftermath of blissful satiation?

Jodie glared, revising her thoughts radically. He couldn't—shouldn't—mourn a dead woman for the rest of his life. He needed someone alive and real to help him forget his mistaken infatuation.

Gradually, over time, he needed to learn what lay beyond sex, what was better than a cold and empty fantasy. He needed to be loved, to find love. Her heart sang. She knew just the woman for the job!

She groaned inwardly, terrified of the emotional risks she was contemplating. This was crazy! He was talking about wanting sex with her for comfort, whereas she was imagining something more profound...

But what did he know? she argued. He was confused, clinging to his shrine to the unattained and unattainable Teresa, consumed with guilt because he hadn't loved Jack's mother as he should have done. But that was in the past.

'Do you *want* me to go?' she purred.

He hesitated, and in that moment she knew the answer. 'I...like having you around,' he said slowly. 'I can hardly deny that, can I? But I'm not blind to the explosive potential of two needy people in close proximity to one another—and I think you should protect yourself from a possibly awkward situation. You don't want a relationship based on sex. We'd quarrel—and our hostility to one another would become obvious. We don't want your father to detect an atmosphere between us.'

'No,' she said. 'For his sake we must be friends. And surely he'd think it odd if I stayed anywhere other than his house? If we're to share the next difficult months then I need to get to know you, Morgan. I think you want that too.'

Morgan opened his mouth to reply and then he let out a groan, leaping out of his chair and flinging the oven door open. Smoke billowed out. Jodie went over and they both stood there staring in surprise at the blackened remains of the pizza.

'I don't believe it!' he exclaimed irritably.

'Easy to do.' A smile tipped the corners of her mouth. 'What with your cooking and mine, we'll be as skinny as string in no time at all!'

His lips twitched and he gave a rueful grin. 'I've never done that before!'

She laughed, watching him lift out the remains and slam the heavy iron door shut. 'Join the club. I'm an old hand.'

'You're teaching me bad tricks,' he admonished, scraping the mess into the bin.

'I've got plenty more up my sleeve.'

He drew away, his mouth pinching in. 'That's what worries me. I don't know that I can be what you want, Jodie.'

'You couldn't be my friend?' she asked, disappointed. It was the first essential step to a lasting relationship; any idiot knew that.

'That would be the easy part,' he admitted. She beamed and he shook his head in amused exasperation. 'You never give up, do you? I've never met anyone as persuasive.'

'People where I worked used to say I could sell pork pies to vegetarians,' she said, her eyes dancing with hope.

Morgan groaned. 'Don't talk about food! I'm starving. Look…we need time to think this over. Shall we put a hold on any decisions for the moment and go to the pub first?' he suggested.

A reprieve. Glad that their row had blown over, she nodded. 'And Jack?'

'I can bundle him up and bring him too. There's a children's area—though it'll be fairly quiet at this time of night. What do you say?'

'I say, why not?' she agreed happily.

Things were moving on, she thought, hugging herself in delight. Morgan had admitted they could be good friends. It was a promising start.

From the house it was only a short walk to the pub. When he opened the door she walked in to a cheerful atmosphere full of noise and chatter, which abated when they were noticed and then increased considerably in volume.

'We're being discussed,' he muttered under his breath.

'It's tempting to do something outrageous,' she whispered with a wicked grin.

He looked at her mouth, as if contemplating landing a kiss there. 'I could order champagne and feed you oysters with my teeth.'

She made a face. 'I'd rather have steak pie and chips.'

'The gravy would drip down my chin.'

Jodie raised an eyebrow. 'No problem. There's a bib in your pocket with hedgehogs on it.'

'So there is,' he cried, rummaging for it.

'No! Don't!' she giggled, going pink at the sideways glances from everyone.

'If you insist. Performance over, then. Let's head for the family room,' Morgan proposed.

Family room, she thought sentimentally, and sighed. It was small and empty, but bright with balloons and a colourful rack of children's books and jigsaws. Outside she could see a floodlit garden with a climbing frame and a slide.

Relaxing by the log fire, Jodie enjoyed her experience of

an English pub. She and Morgan chatted all through the meal, though later she couldn't remember what they'd talked about—only that his eyes had never left hers and she'd felt a wild and uncontainable joy.

'Ready to leave?' he asked suddenly.

'Oh, must we go?' She didn't want their companionship to end. Going back would break the spell. 'I like it here. It's cosy.'

'I like it too, but I'm working on baby hours,' he said with a wry smile. 'Jack hauls me out of bed a few times in the night and I need to get some sleep in first.' He stood up. 'OK, force me. One quick half and then we must leave. I'd love to stay longer, but—'

'I understand. We can't have everything we want, can we?'

Morgan froze. Jodie had been on his mind all evening. Jodie and Jack. Something flicked into his mind, a fleeting, crazy thought that flung his resolution into disarray.

'What did you say?' he breathed.

She looked up at him and blinked. 'OK, so it was a trite cliché But it's true. We can never have everything we want.'

His head came up and he stared ahead sightlessly. 'Can't we?' he murmured, a smile curving his masculine mouth.

'You know we can't,' she replied in a sad voice.

But they could. His heart thundered in his chest. 'Two halves of cider coming up,' he said, excitement hurtling through him.

Morgan strode to the bar and waited to be served, his mind whirling with the rapidity of events. All his life he'd had a strength of will that was phenomenal: admired, feared and discussed with awe by friends and colleagues.

With Jodie he could only respond to his basic instincts.

Or perhaps, he mused, some higher command that knew what was right for him.

He liked and admired her. Found himself unable to stop touching her. And she felt the same way about him. All evening they'd talked like old friends. He hadn't imagined the look in her eyes. She was naturally wary, and afraid of being used, but she wasn't the sort of woman to opt for sex without a deeper emotion backing it up.

Could they make a go of a relationship? It was crucial that they did. He licked dry lips, conscious that his lungs were deprived of air. Slowly he brought his breathing under control. He would test the water. Court her. And when the time was right, he'd make love to her. And then he'd propose.

'Yes?'

He stared blankly at the woman behind the bar and then smiled. 'Sorry. Miles away. Two halves of cider, please.'

He opened his wallet and extracted a note, elation rippling through him. He grinned at the woman. 'And one for yourself.'

He could have everything he wanted. Jodie and Jack. He'd found the solution.

His gaze fell on the small packet tucked in the back of his wallet—forgotten since his liaison with Teresa. He stared at it, knowing it gave him the opportunity to make love to Jodie without the danger of a pregnancy.

Dangerous. He was teetering on the brink of a precipice—virtually ready to throw himself over!

Turning, he saw her pensively smiling into space and strode forward, recklessly disregarding caution and more than ready to take the plunge.

They fell into a comfortable routine very quickly—almost like a married couple, Jodie thought happily as she

Hoovered the stairs with loving care.

Since the evening at the pub Morgan had been relaxed and friendly, and despite their worries about her father there had been moments of laughter and a deep contentment that she had never known before.

Morgan concentrated on Jack, she looked after the house, and they both did the shopping and cooking. He'd begun to work in his study, leaving the door open so, he said in a hopeful hint, she could wander in with cups of tea.

Taking him at his word, she brought a pot of tea and chocolate cake one afternoon, pausing to admire the drawing he was finishing.

'That looks like a church!' she exclaimed, placing the tray on his desk.

He swivelled around from the drawing slope. 'It is. Look…I'm really excited about this.'

Encouraged, she came closer. '"St Bartholomew's",' she read. 'You're designing a church?'

He laughed. 'No! Better than that. Converting it. The bishop has decided it's too large for the congregation and most of it is wasted. So I'm dividing it in half.'

He flicked over a sheet. She looked at him and adored him. He was so happy, so absorbed in his work. With a sigh she dragged her gaze from his eager face and tried to make out the drawing.

'Looks like a hotel,' she said, puzzled.

'Close. A hostel—for the homeless.' He put his arm around her shoulders, drawing her even nearer. 'Look, Jodie. It's a brilliant idea. There's a day room, kitchens to cook their meals, and small, individual rooms for thirty people. I've had to tuck them into the church arches, but it works, don't you think?'

She beamed, thrilled with the idea. 'It's wonderful. Oh

Morgan, you must be so proud to be doing something that's such a benefit to the community!'

He smiled back. 'I am,' he said softly. 'I feel I'm putting something back. I want to see where else this can be done. The only thing stopping this happening all over the country is lack of funding. The bishop wants local firms to contribute—'

'I could help there!' she said with a laugh. 'I sell pork pies to vegetarians, remember?'

'Would you?' He caught her arms, his eyes searching hers as if he hardly dared to believe her commitment. 'Jodie... We could set this up. You could meet the bishop, make contact with the Chamber of Commerce—'

'I'd love to!' she said, dizzy with happiness.

'Jodie.' He kissed her hard. Then drew back. 'Sorry! But...I'm pleased,' he said more soberly.

She forced herself to calm down too. Lifting an eyebrow, she said, 'I hadn't noticed.'

And, nonchalant to a fault, she sauntered over to the tea tray and cut herself a slice of cake. But inside she was fizzing with delight. They were becoming closer than she'd dared to hope. And now she would be working on something that enthused them both.

Later that day they had their usual walk. She skipped along beside him, chattering away, holding his hand and loving its warm, dry enclosure. And a while after he even allowed her to help bath Jack, an honour she valued more than anything.

Under Morgan's guidance she undressed the baby and learnt how to hold him safely, her happiness almost complete.

'It's been a lovely day,' she said softly, when they both tiptoed out of the nursery. 'I've enjoyed every single moment.'

'Coffee?'

She should refuse. Offer a friendly smile and take the newspaper to bed. But she wanted him desperately and the flesh was weak.

'OK,' she said recklessly, hoping her croak sounded vaguely casual.

In the drawing room, softly lit by candles, he poured the coffee and she felt her hunger rising. Her fingers itched to trace his smooth jaw; her mouth quivered in expectation of exploring the golden skin between collar and hairline. And that tempting dark taper of hair in front of his ear...

He stood in front of her, gazing down. The liquid was slopping in the cups he held.

'It's not going to work,' he said thickly, his eyes burning through her fevered body.

'What?' she pretended, her voice hardly hers.

'If you want us to be friends and nothing else then you must go to bed now,' he warned, his deep voice soft as a whisper, flowing over her like liquid velvet.

She couldn't move. Didn't want to. She knew full well what he meant—and what would happen if she remained.

'Trouble is, I'm not sleepy,' she breathed.

He grunted. 'I keep thinking of you and bed—and sleep doesn't figure in the equation at all,' he said huskily.

'We can't fight the inevitable, Morgan,' she murmured.

'I feel I should try.'

'Not on my account.'

He drew in a sharp breath. 'Jodie! This is beyond me! I can't think, can't behave normally when you're around. You're in my head and in my body and I think I'll go mad if I can't touch you!'

In answer, she lifted her face, her lips parted avidly for his kiss. The pain of her passion etched itself in her eyes and through her entire body as she waited for the inevitable.

Slowly, without taking his eyes off her, he put down the two cups and knelt in front of her. His fingers lightly smoothed over her hands where they lay on her knees. And then he was pressing his mouth to each palm, first one and then the other, his bone structure infinitely beautiful in the flickering firelight.

Adoring him, she surrendered everything—caution, sense, security, restraint. 'Morgan,' she purred, and slid to the floor, her skirts pooling around her.

'I can't believe I'm doing this!' he said, looking dazed.

'We tried. We did our best to talk ourselves out of it. Who can stop the urging of fate?'

'I don't want you to think that I—'

She stopped him, her finger on his protesting lips. 'No thinking.'

He kissed her fingertip, his eyes burning. 'Hear me out. It's not just sex. Not just comfort.'

Love flowed through her, melting her very bones. 'I know,' she whispered. 'Or I wouldn't be here.'

'No going back this time.'

'No...'

His hand brushed back her hair. His lips touched her forehead, her temple, and the pulse in front of her ear. And she sat there shuddering as if he had spent an hour arousing her instead of a second or two, every part of her alive and humming with electricity, her heart throbbing with happiness.

A finger caressed her mouth. With a groan she took the finger between her teeth and nibbled gently, moaning as her need filled every cell of her body. His mouth came down hard on hers, pushing her back till she lay on the floor, moving like a temptress.

'I want you...' he growled.

She jerked with longing. 'Yes.'

'I shouldn't—'

Impatiently she pushed him away and slid back, a feeling of intense satisfaction rippling through her when he stared at her, appalled, his chest heaving hard.

Lowering her head and flirting with him from beneath her brows, she shimmied out of her dress, exulting in Morgan's inhalation of breath when he realised what she was doing.

'No,' she agreed provocatively. 'You shouldn't. I shouldn't.' She moistened her lips and unhooked her bra. 'Stay!' she ordered when he made an involuntary movement towards her. She smoothed her hands over her breasts, watching his tortured face. He'd never forget her, she thought exultantly, reaching for his hands. 'Touch,' she whispered.

Instead, his tongue slipped wickedly around one turgid nipple, making her buck as the needle spasms flicked like lightning through her body. Her eyes closed as tiny thrills built upon one another, driving her crazy with impatience.

His actions told her that he felt the same. Roughly he stripped off his clothes and slid away her briefs. He was beautiful. His sheer masculinity took her breath away. He wanted her.

Hot-eyed and intent, he let his hands move over her shivering skin—curving around her breasts, enjoying their firmness, finger and thumb tantalising the hot, dark centres.

Her back arched, demanding in the only way she knew how that he satisfied the desperate emptiness within her. She couldn't speak, could barely move her leaden limbs, all her mind obliterated by everything but that one fierce need.

Obeying some deep and primal message, she bent her head and tasted him…heat, silk and throbbing muscle slithering in her warm, moist mouth in a heady combination.

Morgan groaned, close to losing control. He muttered something to her, gently but firmly lifting her away. He wanted this to be for her. To give her something he'd never shared before. His whole self.

'Jodie!' he husked, his eyes brilliantly intense. 'Come here!'

His mouth devoured hers. She felt soft and giving beneath him and he ground his body against hers, letting himself slide against the warm, welcoming tremble of her pelvis.

Their tongues meshed, mimicking what they both desired. A rhythm beat in his pulses, his heart, the movement of their tongues, their hips. He rolled away slightly to allow his hand to explore, hushing her when she jerked and cried out, whimpering and panting as he relentlessly moved a delicate finger across the wet, firm nub between her legs.

Jodie thrashed around, her hair skimming out like burnished gold, her face more beautiful than he could believe possible. He covered it with kisses, suckled her breasts with a tender ferocity, his hands, arms, legs trapping her, forcing her to accept his caresses as the velvet of her skin and the receptive moistness of her body under his fingers built up a friction and a promise that he could no longer refuse.

She seemed possessed. Beneath him her body writhed and lured, the flick of her nipples across his chest infinitely pleasurable. Without inhibition she had parted her legs for him and was intent on slipping her hand to his waiting shaft.

But he stopped her, knowing he couldn't hold back if she did.

'Wait,' he muttered.

'Won't!' she scowled.

'You'll like it better if you do,' he murmured shakily. Angrily she lurched against his fingers, her eyes dark

with frustration. Her sleek hair whispered over his breast-
bone as she leaned forwards and nibbled ruthlessly at his
nipple.

She wouldn't wait much longer. Nor could he. Her hands
were raking across his back and there was a desperate fury
in the sinuous demands of her body. Briefly he reached out,
searching for what he needed. Now he was safe—and she
too.

'I'm ready for you. Is this what you want?' he whispered.

He allowed himself just to touch the entrance to her
body, his hands holding her back. But she flashed him one
siren look and jerked her hips in a swift movement, her
silky heat enclosing him with a suddenness that left him
gasping.

And she groaned with him, a long, urgent release of
long-held passion. His bones seemed to melt. Something
painful jerked in his heart and he found himself totally unaware of where he was; he felt as if he was floating, slipping slowly and inexorably into paradise.

'Watch me,' she moaned.

He realised his eyes had closed. With difficulty he
opened them and saw her fevered face, her gaze intent on
the intermingling dark and chestnut coils of hair where their
bodies met.

Amazed at what that sight did to him, he found himself
thrusting, incapable of restraining himself any longer. And
she looked, crying, moaning like him, fiercely intensifying
each stroke with the supple thrusts of her own impassioned
body.

For a moment he stopped, knowing that the pause would
heighten her orgasm. She glared, grabbed his head and
kissed him till he felt the pressure of exquisite torture exploding within him.

'Don't stop!' she ordered, her thready voice trembling.

He wanted to make this last. To imprint this moment on her. Hot and hungry, he stemmed his own need and concentrated on kissing her while she did everything she could to entice him onwards.

Sweat slicked on their bodies and she licked at him with her cat-like tongue, causing his skin to shiver and tremble as every nerve responded. He felt the edge of her teeth as frustration drove her to more desperate measures and so he moved again, with the utmost leisure, each gliding movement making him hotter, more swollen, more violently sensitive to her sweetness.

In the back of his dazed mind he was afraid that he would hurt her, but she surged against him and clung with such greed that he banished that fear from his mind, and in a moment of extreme emotion he kissed her tenderly, then increased the tempo of his body.

Jodie whispered with delight, her eyes sparkling as she gazed at him as if... He faltered, then, urged by her frantic writhing, drove firmly into her... As if...she loved him, he thought.

Morgan cried out loud, their rhythm hot and fast, bodies as one, hearts, minds, emotions...who knew? He couldn't think, only his senses were operating, and most of those were focused on the slippery heat in the core of her body.

'Morgan!' she gasped, gripping his shoulders. Her head rolled back, her throat creamy and smooth.

He kissed the pulse there, murmured words...silly words, telling her she was wonderful, beautiful, wicked, luscious...

And then they both shouted, clinging to one another as the violence of their orgasms crashed through them. For the first time he felt the incredible force of her contractions as they squeezed and released the intensely sensitive shaft deep within her. It was a moment of astounding pleasure

that almost drove him into orbit as each wave rolled
through and around him, the whole of his body seemingly
one giant organ of gratification.

It lasted for ever. Hours. Almost as soon as she subsided,
with little sighs of deep satisfaction, he was aroused again.
Her eyes opened wide in amazement as he began to move.
A smile curved her sensual mouth and he smiled back, his
eyes glittering with excitement.

This was something else. Something special. He felt like
a god. Invincible, all-powerful, able to pleasure his woman.
He could no more stop himself from giving himself what
he wanted than he could stop breathing.

Gently he hauled her onto his lap. The firm peaks of her
breasts swung to him in supplication and he took each in
his mouth in turn, savouring the sweetness of them and
revelling in what it did to her.

'Ride me,' he muttered.

She stretched her lovely body, and in that moment when
she looked at him, her eyes soft and adoring, he felt a
crushing sensation in his heart.

'Jodie.' His ragged attempt to articulate his volcanic
emotions failed as she slid onto him, her mouth insistent
on his.

She swayed, twisting so erotically that he couldn't think
at all. There was only the proud carriage of her ribcage, the
hollow beneath and the tiny waist, the shine of sweat on
her honey skin and the unbelievable fire burning in his
loins.

Through half-closed eyes he watched her come, thrilled
at her abandon and the wantonness of her frenzied hands
as they clutched at his hard, tight buttocks and forced him
deeper into her. He slid with agonising exhilaration into
that darkness again, where the pleasure was in his head and

in his manhood for one magnificent explosion, before rocketing fiercely into every vein and nerve he possessed.

His arms enfolded her lovingly. He held her close to him, her face nuzzled in his neck and his in hers. Inhaling her. His lips pressed to her salty skin, feeling the heat, the satiny fire that quivered and leapt across her entire body as aftershocks trembled through them both.

'Jodie.'

She stirred, but otherwise remained limp in his arms. 'Mmm.'

''Swonderful.' He was slurred. His mouth didn't match up with his brain.

'Mmm.'

Her arms tightened around his neck. Conscious that she might soon be cold, when their heated bodies cooled down, he slid her into his arms and staggered for a moment, then found his balance and strength.

He looked down at her blissful face and knew he was smiling idiotically. 'Bed.'

'Mmm.'

Trustingly she snuggled against his naked chest. He felt like a king. Carrying his precious burden, he made it up the stairs and to his room, his heart thudding so loudly that it alarmed him.

'Shower,' she mumbled.

His loins stirred. 'Shower,' he agreed hoarsely.

He set her on her feet and closed the cabinet door. His shower was vast, the showerhead enormous. Lovingly he supported her wilting body, seeing that she was barely aware of what was happening. She seemed to be where he was—on Cloud Nine, he thought with a smile.

The water cascaded over them and he gently smoothed his gel-soaked palms over her glorious dips and curves. She raised her arms in the air in a sensual stretch and took the gel from the rack. He closed his eyes.

The feel of her fingers exploring each muscle of his shoulders was tantalising in the extreme. Her wet thumb dipped into the hollow of his collarbone. Anticipation set him on fire.

'Oh, Morgan! You're just greedy!' she breathed.

'I can't help it,' he said jerkily. 'I only have to look at you to want you! And this...is more than I can bear!'

Her hands massaged his spine and splayed out to his hips, and he was acutely aware of where he wanted her to touch next. Hungry, he reached out to touch her, but she slapped him down.

'My turn,' she murmured.

And then he rocked on his feet as she knelt, the wet pelt of her hair against his pelvis as she took him in her mouth again, and he felt the pressure increase as her lips slid up and down with a sure skill and sensitivity which came close to driving him insane with ecstasy.

But as she suckled he found it wasn't enough. He wanted to be with her. In her. His hand snapped off the shower. He ignored her protests, wrapped her in an enormous warm bath towel and gently, sensually dried her. Paying close and extended attention to her most erotic areas.

'Bed,' he purred when they were both dry and she was trembling with need.

'Mmm!' she squeaked.

They lay together, looking at one another for a long time. Jodie felt as if her heart had stopped. She loved him. Really loved him.

Gently they explored, learning one another. She felt a great happiness steal over her. Euphoria alternated with elation and then settled on her in a deep serenity. He was smiling, his whole face alight with joy.

She had done it, she thought, hardly daring to believe it. Morgan had come out of mourning. He'd found someone of flesh and bone and their coming together had been little short of miraculous.

Everything between them had resonated with deeper vibrations. This hadn't been pure sex. It had been a celebration of two people passionately involved in one another, two hearts beating as one.

She knew that from the way he looked at her now, in a bemused, dazzled, wonderfully amazed delight.

Their lovemaking was gentle and slow this time. Each movement Morgan made was considered and yet deliciously tentative. They knew one another. Her fingers unerringly descended on a muscle here, a pulse there. His head swooped directly to her breast...to the tiny wet bud between her legs.

Luxuriantly she relaxed every muscle, while the heat of his mouth prepared her. And then with one accord they moved to one another, her heart soaring as he took her beyond any place she'd ever visited, far away to where her love could expand and fill her body and every movement of her hands, every breath she took and every sigh that escaped her bruised mouth.

After, they clung to one another, as if fearful that it had all been a dream. And slowly it became just that: their muscles easing, their heartbeats slowing from their hectic rhythms, their expressions serene and peaceful.

CHAPTER NINE

SHE woke in the night, her hand sleepily reaching out for him. It encountered just the rumpled sheet.

'Morgan?' she mumbled, disorientated.

A kiss brushed her cheek and she saw his dim figure looming over her.

'Baby's awake. Back later.'

'Whosstime?' she mumbled drowsily.

'Three a.m. Go to sleep, sweetheart,' he whispered.

Sweetheart. She sighed with satisfaction and must have dozed, because when she stirred again the room was lighter. Rolling over, she saw Morgan lying beside her, his eyes liquid ink. She smiled and snuggled up.

'Ohh! You're as cold as ice!' she gasped.

'Took a long time to bring up Jack's wind. Another five minutes and he'll be ready for his next feed again!'

Jodie craned her neck. It was five-twenty. 'You must be exhausted,' she sympathised. 'You do need a nanny—'

'No! I look after Jack!' he said forcibly. 'No one else!'

'Then let me warm you. And for heaven's sake, get some sleep now,' she replied, touched by his devotion.

It was wonderful watching him relax in her arms. Slowly the dark lashes fluttered down and his features softened. Her heart turned over when she contemplated the soft arch of his sensual mouth and she couldn't resist touching it with a delicate forefinger.

He murmured in his sleep and nuzzled his face in her neck. She stroked his hair and wondered about the future. Lying there, she pictured herself with Morgan and Jack, watching the baby grow into a toddler, a schoolchild, a young adult. Her head swam with the heady delight of being part of a loving family.

Her father would be thrilled, she thought. He patently adored Morgan and nothing would give him greater pleasure than to know that she and Morgan had found happiness together.

She stroked Morgan's hair, imprinting every line, every angle of his face on her memory.

'I love you,' she whispered, kissing his forehead softly.

His eyes snapped open and she jerked back in confusion. Beneath her hand, his shoulder muscles had tensed into a hard knot.

'What was that?' he asked in a low rumble.

She pressed her treacherous lips together, her eyes startled and anxious. Morgan fixed her with his penetrating gaze and heaved himself up on one elbow.

'Cat got your tongue?' he murmured.

She put it out. 'You were supposed to be asleep,' she accused.

'I was.' His eyes twinkled. 'Something filtered through to my subconscious. Something I've been wanting to hear.'

She sat bolt upright. 'What?'

A dazzling smile. A laugh of triumph. An amused shake of his head. 'Oh, Jodie!' he said fondly. 'You don't know how I feel at this moment!' Laughingly he pinned her back on the pillows, kissing her till she could hardly breathe. 'Tell me what you said,' he demanded. And when she remained mute he kissed her again, harder, demanding to know again and again till she surrendered.

'OK, OK!' she complained. 'You're giving me stubble burn!'

Her hand caressed the side of his face, scratching at the bristles. He looked like a sexy gypsy, wild and rough and dangerous—even if she knew he was kind and gentle and thoughtful. Though, she mused, a spark of desire fizzling through her, he could be sexy and wild...

'You're stalling,' he warned, with a ferociously theatrical scowl.

Jodie giggled. 'Just diverted by something.'

'Get back on track,' he growled, pretending to be angry.

'I said,' she breathed, kissing his grumpy mouth till it curved up into a smile again, 'that I love you.'

His eyes closed. He remained as if frozen. She waited, tension stringing out her nerves, robbing her heart of its normal beat. Afraid, she swallowed. Had she spoken too soon?

'Are you sure?' he asked eventually, his voice shaking with emotion.

'I fell in love with you almost at once,' she said simply. 'I didn't believe that could happen, but it did. And, yes, now I'm sure.'

His mouth touched hers tentatively in a delicate kiss. Then his lips brushed her brow. 'Jodie,' he said, very serious, 'I could be rushing you...but I am compelled to speak my feelings—'

'Yes?' She held her breath, waiting for him to declare his love too. She was so certain of it.

'It's only been a short time that we've known one another,' he said huskily. 'But we seem to be in total harmony. I am...so happy when you're around. I can't imagine what it would be like to live apart from you. I want you to be my wife. Marry me, Jodie. Make it soon. Let's be together for the rest of our lives.'

She gave a sob and reached up her arms to him. 'Yes!' she cried, her eyes awash with tears. 'Yes, Morgan!'

His kisses deepened. She felt the tip of his tongue tasting her tears, the warmth of his mouth moving over her face.

Flames leapt through her and she groaned, sliding her body against his for the union which would seal their pact.

And then he was moving away.

'What...? Why...?' she moaned.

'Jack,' he rasped.

'I don't hear him!' she pouted.

'You're not tuned to him,' he replied, dropping a hasty kiss on her nose and flicking off the baby alarm.

Denied and empty, she lay crossly in bed, and then felt selfish and mean for resenting a needy baby even for a few seconds. She leapt up, slipping on her thin cotton robe, and hurried to the nursery, intending to see if she could help in any way.

'Oh, God!' she heard him mutter.

She paused just outside the door, surprised by Morgan's impassioned growl. Her senses might not be tuned to the baby, but they were acute where Morgan was concerned. And he seemed to be in a highly emotional state.

'You're safe!' she heard him say jerkily. 'You're mine!' He let out a loud and protracted sigh, as if every part of his body had been under tension for a long, long time. 'Hold on, sweetpea,' he husked, when Jack whimpered. 'It's coming.' Jodie heard Morgan's bare feet striding hard and fast up and down the room. 'We'll be together. No one will take you from me. Never, never, never!'

Jodie clung to the doorjamb, stunned by what she'd heard. He was talking to Jack now, promising him a rosy future, walks in the snow, swimming lessons, riotous birthday parties...

She gulped. None of these seemed to include her. Confused and muddled, she quietly returned to the bedroom. Six-thirty. Suddenly cold, she showered and scrambled into a pair of yellow jeans and a warm orange jumper.

Her confidence had vanished. She didn't feel so sure of

Morgan. Why had he been so relieved after she'd agreed to marry him? His reaction had been more than male pride, or relief that he hadn't been rejected.

And where did Jack come into this? It didn't make sense that Morgan felt his son was safe now. Who would have taken his baby away from him?

Questions filled her head, making it ache. She went down to the kitchen and made some lemon tea, then put it down, too sick to her stomach to take even that. So she found a pill in the first aid box and took it for her headache.

Fear had suddenly entered her life, spoiling her brief moment of pure joy. There was something dark and threatening lurking in the background, waiting to snatch happiness from her grasp.

And she couldn't, wouldn't interrogate Morgan, for fear that she would arouse a sleeping tiger.

All that day she remained curled up on the sofa with a blinding headache, tended by a concerned and sympathetic Morgan. He was so thoughtful and loving that she could almost believe she must have imagined what she'd heard.

He'd always been over-protective towards Jack. Although she adored him, and dearly wanted to take a larger part in Jack's care, she'd never been allowed to feed him, nor had Morgan ever left her in sole charge of the baby. Perhaps that was just a natural parenting instinct.

She perked up. Perhaps Morgan just felt more secure with the prospect of having a wife. Despite political correctness, it was still unusual for a father to bring up a child alone—especially a tiny baby. Maybe Social Services had expressed doubts as to his ability and he'd felt threatened.

'I'm glad to see you smiling again.' He stood in the doorway, a warm smile lighting his face. And she was sure there was love in his eyes.

'I love you,' she said fervently, ashamed that she'd doubted him for one moment.

'Oh, Jodie!' He came to her, knelt and held her tightly. She could feel him trembling and she hugged him hard. 'We must celebrate our engagement,' he murmured in her ear.

'I could cook!' she suggested, teasing.

'Thanks. I don't want to die yet,' he said drily. 'We should go out. Somewhere special.' He frowned. 'But somewhere we can take Jack—'

'The pub's fine by me,' she said quickly. 'I don't need champagne and waiters with French accents, or designer food sitting on raspberry coulis. All I need is you, Morgan. And Jack too, of course.' She pulled back a little, anxious to reassure him. 'He'll be family, after all.'

His smile touched her heart with its brilliance. 'Yes,' he said throatily. 'He will.' And he enfolded her in his arms again, crushing her to him with such intense passion that she could barely breathe for delight.

Their lovemaking had never been so tender, so sweetly wrung with tremulous emotion. Jodie felt drugged by her feelings, washed by a tide of blissful sensations which made her limbs liquid, her brain dizzy with the intoxication of the deepest love.

She watched him feeding and changing Jack, drowsily amazed at his stamina and energy. No matter how tired he was, how hard a day he'd had—or night—he stayed calm and gentle with his beloved son, and never once did he show impatience or resentment when Jack made his needs known.

Not that the baby cried much. Morgan was always there, interpreting Jack's needs, firmly and competently coping with his son. And she adored Morgan all the more for that, thinking ahead to the time when they would have babies of their own.

Later, when they were settled in their favourite corner of the pub by the fire, Morgan took her hand in his and said gently, 'To us. To our marriage.' He lowered his lashes and said, almost under his breath, 'To the woman I adore best in the world.'

Her heart turned over. 'Oh, Morgan!' she mumbled, tears of happiness shining in her eyes. 'To us,' she responded. 'The man I adore and will love always.'

'We'll go out tomorrow and choose a ring. Name the day. Make arrangements.'

She smiled shyly. 'I'd love that.'

'And there's something else. I kept a piece of news back for you. Sam's going to the nursing home tomorrow. I think perhaps next week—when he's settled in—would be a good time to talk to him about you. I'm sure he'll be eager to meet you when I've told him the kind of person you are.'

'Heavens! Don't do that—he'll run a mile!' she said with a laugh.

'I could make it up,' he offered, his eyes twinkling. 'Tell him you're a slick city girl with a computer for a brain—'

'But kind to ferrets and gerbils—'

'Sure.' He grinned, pretending to shade his eyes when he looked at her. 'And who dresses...' he did a mock wince '...soberly—'

'And who's always calm and collected!' Jodie beamed. She enjoyed his teasing. Chas had teased. But it had been cruel and goading. Morgan did it in a loving way. She gave a contented sigh. 'You've made my day complete,' she said. 'I can't wait to see my father—'

'Jodie...' He hesitated. 'I have something rather difficult to say. It's about Jack.'

She froze. Suddenly Morgan seemed distant and withdrawn, his body language speaking volumes. 'Are you in danger of losing him?' she asked, voicing his fears.

His head jerked up. 'What the hell do you mean?' he demanded roughly.

'I—I don't know, it's just that I wondered…you seemed worried… Jack's so important to you…' Her voice faded under his savage frown. Her hand felt limp and shaky and she put her glass of Château Lafite down hurriedly. Morgan was on the defensive. She'd made a mistake. 'Forget it. A stab in the dark. Silly—'

'OK.' He waved an impatient hand at her incoherent gabble and she subsided, hurt and on edge. She waited while he sat there, chewing over the words he intended to say, alarmed by his tense expression. 'You know I've…looked after Jack ever since he was born.'

She waited again. He seemed stuck, so she decided to encourage him. 'I admire you for that commitment. And you've become welded to him because his mother left—'

'She didn't leave.' His eyes met hers, hard, unfathomable. 'She died.' And before she could express sympathy he went on, his voice rough and grating. 'Jack is Teresa's child.'

'Teresa's?' Jodie sat rooted to her chair in shock. 'I thought…' Her brow furrowed deeply as she tried to make sense of what he was saying. 'But…Teresa was my *father's* lover.'

'Yes.' Morgan licked his lips, picked up his wine and put it down again. 'Of course when Sam was taken ill he couldn't take over his role as…' Morgan lifted his glass again and took a long gulp of claret. 'As Jack's father,' he said, oddly hoarse. 'So I took over.'

'Jack…is Sam and Teresa's baby?' she said stupidly.

'He was thrilled to know she was pregnant,' he said, pursuing his own train of thought. But the smile he flashed at her wasn't quite right and there was an odd sharpness to his cheekbones, which were standing high in his strained face. 'I think if it hadn't been for Jack your father might have given up the fight to live long ago,' he finished stiffly.

Her brain didn't seem to be functioning. Why all this should chill her to the bone she didn't know, but she felt shivers running up and down her spine. She stretched out her hands to the fire, glad to be avoiding Morgan's hunted eyes.

What was the matter? Why was he walking on pins? Injecting as much normality into her tone as she could, she said, 'It's a bit of a shock to learn this, Morgan. Why didn't you tell me earlier?'

'Because you might not have stayed. Until I was certain that you would—and that you were committed to Sam—I didn't want your decision to be swayed by an appealing little baby half-brother.'

She turned and fixed him with a worried stare. 'Any more surprises?' she asked shakily, wondering why she didn't entirely accept this reason.

'Teresa is Jack's mother. I swear that is the truth, on Jack's head.'

Again he hadn't answered her question directly. Her heart sank. Was that why Morgan loved the baby so? Did Jack look like Teresa? Was Morgan hoping—longing, maybe—for Jack to grow up reminding him of the woman he'd loved with such an extraordinary passion?

Her breath hissed in. 'Excuse me,' she said. 'Need the Ladies'.'

He caught her hand as she made to leave. 'I want you to know that I did what was best,' he said quietly.

He was a good man. She smiled because she loved him, but she was hurting inside. 'You're taking care of a motherless baby whose father is seriously ill. Anyone would admire you for that,' she told him in a low tone. 'Must dash!'

Her grin faded once she'd reached the safety of the cloakroom. She patted her hot, flushed face with cold water and held her wrists under the tap. In the mirror she saw a woman who'd fallen in love with a man who was still tied to someone else. Tied, too, to that woman's baby.

Of course he loved Jack. Anybody would. She herself adored him, loved his little fingers—builder's hands, Morgan had said outrageously—and his sweetly peaceful face when he slept, the dark mat of hair and his warm, baby smell. And Morgan was a decent, wonderful man to devote himself to the baby.

This was her half-brother. Her hands stilled as a bond sprang up which had not been there before. Awed, she realised that she now had responsibilities, duties towards Jack.

But…Teresa's child!

Jodie groaned and swayed, nausea hitting the pit of her stomach. Her mind whirled, trying to make sense of the new situation.

There was no blood link between Jack and Morgan—only a deep and unbreakable love. Her father was Jack's next of kin.

Numbly she stared at herself in the mirror, her eyes widening as her mind raced on, setting things in place.

Morgan knew that her father only had a short time to live. And he was obviously aware that she would soon be Jack's next of kin. In law, she would be responsible for Jack.

Her hands shook. Morgan had become firmly attached to Jack—almost over-possessive. Was this, perhaps, why Morgan had been so hostile? Why he'd tried to send her away? And why he'd kept Jack's parentage a secret from her until now?

Something else occurred to her. A thought so unspeakable that she pushed it back in horror. 'Please, no!' she whispered, aghast. 'He loves me! He really loves me!'

She would *not* believe that she could be so wrong about someone. Morgan wouldn't have proposed to her just to secure his link with Jack!

'No!' she said fiercely to the doubting woman in the mirror. 'He's kind and he's loving and every part of me knows that!'

Be careful, the eyes of the woman said. Be cautious.

With a wounded cry, Jodie fled, desperately banishing her doubts. Morgan loved her. She would make sure of that.

And later that night she wove a spell over him, teasing, tantalising, luring him with her mind and body and soul, all her intense passions and fears focused on arousing his love.

Once or twice, in the back of her mind, she wondered if he was thinking of Teresa during their most intimate moments. And in those brief seconds she felt her heart would crack in two.

'Love me,' she murmured passionately.

His eyes closed in bliss, Morgan took her lower lip in his mouth, tasting its swollen softness. Jodie's passion more than matched his own, flinging him into the deepest pool of ecstasy he could ever have imagined.

He slid his tongue to her teeth and she immediately allowed him entrance into the dark, warm moistness. Their tongues meshed and fierce stabs of need scythed through his loins.

She felt soft and pliable, her lissom body moving with agonising seductiveness against his, her eyes knowing and excitingly wicked.

He nuzzled her throat and the slender collarbone while

his knee parted her legs and his hands enjoyed the firm lushness of her high, rounded breasts.

He groaned and, dipping his head, he greedily lapped at each thrusting nipple, loving the smell of her, the warmth of her satin skin against his face, the sensual feel of the hard, engorged peak in his mouth as it jerked in response to his impassioned suckling.

'What are you thinking?' she asked in a shaky little voice.

For a moment he couldn't get his head around that. 'Of you!' he croaked.

She seemed to shudder throughout the length of her body and he looked up at her in surprise. Huge tears were seeping from her tightly shut eyes.

'Jodie!' He was holding her, cradling her head against his chest, then kissing and licking away the tears. 'What is it?' he murmured gently.

The enormous liquid green eyes opened. Wet lashes fluttered. 'I'm afraid!' she sobbed.

He drew her close again, stroking her hair. 'Because you think we might not last?' There was the briefest of nods, teardrops wetting his torso. Morgan pushed her back, slid off the bed and came back with a handkerchief. 'Blow,' he instructed. 'Now,' he said when she seemed calmer, 'look at me.' He gazed into those vulnerable eyes and felt his heart cramp. 'For me, marriage is forever. Infidelity is all about opportunity and an attitude of mind. I am a loyal person, Jodie. When I love, I love. I have no intention of ever being anything but devoted to you. If there ever are any hitches in the future then we will work them out, because we are determined that our marriage will last. Trust me. We must not ever separate. Do you believe me when I say that?'

She nodded, though her eyes still looked tragic. 'Yes, I

do. You won't want us to part,' she repeated like an obedient child.

'Come close—'

'No…I feel a bit sick and heady again,' she said in a
forlorn tone. 'I'll just curl up and sleep it off.'

'Of course. Anything I can get you?' he asked in concern.

'No,' she mumbled. 'Let me sleep.'

She seemed fine the next day, though more subdued than
usual, and she didn't want to put off their trip to London
to choose a ring.

Morgan insisted on taking her to an exclusive restaurant
for lunch as a treat—an old haunt of his—so that she could
wave her left hand about a lot. It was good to hear her
laughter when he said this, and he was glad she'd recov-
ered.

Sitting in the restaurant's lounge afterwards feeding Jack,
he leant back in the comfortable chair and watched her
talking to the waiter who'd brought their coffee. He noticed
that she looked the young man in the eye instead of treating
him like an object and addressing his stomach. He liked
that.

'You're staring,' she said in amusement.

'No. Just blinded by you,' he murmured.

'Oh! Blinded?' She looked pleased.

He decided to tease her. 'Mmm. That flashy egg on the
third finger of your left hand is like a car's headlamps on
full beam—'

'How dare you?' She made a face and waggled her hand
in front of his nose. 'It's not an egg. It's a whacking great
diamond and I adore it, so you'd better get used to me
flashing it about.'

'Vulgar,' he pretended. Jack burped and refused the rest

of his bottle. 'Right,' Morgan said. 'I'd better find the Mother and Baby room.'

'It's in the Ladies' cloakroom!' she said with a giggle.

He grunted. 'Equality! Where is it when you need it? I can't go into that gold-tapped flouncy-frilled boudoir!'

'How do you know what it's like?' she asked, grinning at the accuracy of his description. 'Anyway, let me change him. I do know how. He's not going to be scarred for life by my ministrations.'

'No. All right.' He watched her slip the baby bag over her shoulder and then carefully take Jack in her arms. 'Don't forget the wipes. And the cream's—'

'In the front pocket; I know. Honestly, Morgan, I can manage! Inspect everything when I come back and give me marks out of ten! And you can get him regressed by a hypnotist when he's twenty-four, and check that the experience wasn't too traumatic!'

He laughed sheepishly. 'Sorry. Cluck, cluck. Mother hen. Go and do your worst, woman!'

Laughing happily, she made her way to the powder room and the baby-changing area in an inner room beyond. It was empty when she began to lay out the little changing mat, but then she heard the click of high heels as a group of women entered the outer room, and after a while the sounds of handbags being emptied and lipstick applied as they chatted.

Absorbed with Jack, securely on the padded table, she didn't pay much attention to the drawling, languid voice which was holding forth. Until she heard Morgan's name.

'...simply amazed to see him, darling!'

'Not really... Damn!' swore a woman with a screeching voice. 'I've forgotten my mascara. Lend me yours, sweetie... No, he often came here with Teresa. It was his favourite dive when he worked in London.'

'Looking gorgeous as ever, isn't he?' This woman was purring.

'Hunky, darling. And a trillion times better than when we last clapped eyes on him. God!' cried the screecher. 'Was he grieving or what? I thought he'd keel over when they lowered poor T into the ground. I was ready to give mouth to mouth. Never got the chance.' The woman tittered.

Jodie felt paralysed. Her hands stilled as the others acknowledged Morgan's despair. She knew she ought to go out, but Jack wasn't finished, and…and she couldn't face them—or Morgan. He'd brought Teresa here! Angrily she glared at her shaking hands. And her eyes fixated on her engagement ring, the reason for their celebration lunch. Why choose this restaurant of all places? she thought miserably.

'What about his current popsie?' asked the languid one.

'Not his type,' replied the screecher loudly. 'He's always gone for blondes. He'll never get over T. He probably needed his bed warmed. Sexy devil! T said his stamina was phenomenal.'

Jodie bit back a cry. Her fingers fumbled with the nappy. Morgan had slept with Teresa! Or not slept, she amended bitterly. And she hastened with her task, intending to stalk out and shock them all.

'Maybe he needs someone to keep house. He can't go on looking after someone else's baby forever, can he?' simpered the purrer.

Jodie snapped the poppers of Jack's vest. Nearly done, she thought frantically…

'Don't be daft, duckie.' Screecher was in full squawk again. 'Remember I had a nice little gossip with T's daily when T was living with Sam Frazer. The daily found T and

Morgan half naked in his bathroom. That's why she was sacked.'

No. No! Jodie's heart bumped painfully. Almost blinded by angry tears, she was finding it almost impossible to do up the small buttons on the little jacket.

'So it's Morgan's kid!' gasped the drawler.

'God, you're quick, Annabel!' retorted the screecher, as Jodie froze, quite incapable of any action whatsoever. She blocked her ears, but the speaker had a loud and raucous voice and it would have carried across a parade ground. 'What do *you* think? A sick, ageing guy or a virile, healthy one? You know T adored Morgan. She wanted it all, didn't she? Money, and a rich lover who was eternally bound to her because she'd produced his son.'

'She got what she wanted,' sighed the more gentle purrer.

'Huh!' barked the screecher. 'Much good it did her!'

A baby wipe dropped from Jodie's fingers. The women's voices faded into the background as the blood rushed to her head and roared loudly in her ears.

She felt so sick she could hardly stand upright. She pressed her hands to her stomach, willing the nausea to vanish. Wave upon wave of it lurched upwards through her body and only her fierce will kept it back.

Teresa's seductive face and body lurched into her mind. No man could have resisted Teresa's advances, least of all one who loved her. Jodie dragged a whisper of air into her choking lungs. Morgan had slept with Teresa. The woman he'd loved. Perhaps still loved.

Jodie remembered his toast on the day he proposed. *To the woman I adore best in the world.* He could have been raising his glass to Teresa.

She tried to search her memory for a time when Morgan had said 'I love you, Jodie'. And failed.

She'd been used. Again. For sex, comfort, and to ensure that Jack was forever his. Jack, beloved, deeply adored Jack, the result of a passionate affair with her father's fiancée.

Suddenly she needed to see Morgan's face, as if she might find some hint of the truth written there. Her hand flattened on the wall, steadying herself, as she finished dressing Jack and packing the baby bag.

Her eyes were pale with anguish but she applied a slick of lipstick, pinched her cheeks and straightened her hunched, miserable body before walking into the outer room.

Conversation stopped. In the deafening silence, Jodie checked her lipstick unnecessarily and flicked back her hair. She saw that her eyes looked like two glowing dark coals in her pale face.

Unable to speak, she looked at the three women with a bright, mocking smile on her lips and felt she'd won a small victory when they hastily glanced away. With the utmost dignity she swept out of the powder room and into the warmth of the crowded restaurant.

Not able to meet Morgan's eyes yet, she gently placed Jack in his arms.

'All in one piece,' she trilled, though she'd been shattered into fragments.

Morgan laughed, pretending to check. Jack cooed and gurgled and gave a gummy grin which made Jodie's heart somersault. No one could doubt that he loved the baby with all his heart.

Because Jack was his. Because Jack was Teresa's.

She shook uncontrollably, and masked this by fussing with the cushions of her chair then vigorously stirring the coffee he'd begun to pour out when he'd seen her walking towards him.

He smiled his heart-destroying smile, and even in the depths of her anger and misery she felt the terrible lurch of her idiotically romantic heart.

'You deserve a prize,' he murmured lazily.

What? she thought furiously. A medal for stupidity? She stared at the dish of bon-bons blankly, marshalling all her self-control.

'I certainly do,' she muttered, taking four, and ate them quickly to conceal her splintered emotions.

They tasted of cotton wool in her dry, parched mouth. Horror sucked at her heart and lungs, accelerating her pulses and robbing her of breath. Oh, dear God, she couldn't bear this!

'I thought we'd go shopping,' Morgan said. 'Buy up Bond Street.'

There was a jagged rip inside her now. She'd felt so close to him. Had trusted and admired him. But to cover up his own guilt he was fooling them all. These people, herself, *and her father*! So much for Morgan's supposed loyalty. How could he live with himself, knowing what he did?

She surveyed him from beneath her brows. 'I hope you mean that,' she said with a calmness that amazed her. 'Because I'm in a spending mood.'

You swine! she thought. Rat! Worm! Cheat, liar... Her face paled. Morgan was betraying his own flesh and blood. A tiny, defenceless baby.

She saw the women come in, and on an impulse she waved to them. Morgan turned around, stiffening. His eyes narrowed and she saw that his hands had clenched. Guilt, she thought dully.

'Do you know those women?' he demanded abruptly.

She continued to smile, despite feeling ice-cold to the

core. 'They were in the cloakroom,' she answered casually, sipping her coffee. 'What gossips!'

He seemed quite incapable of speaking for a moment. Alarm was written all over his face and she continued to play the contented fiancée while her heart shrivelled to dust.

'What…what were they gossiping about?' he enquired.

'You. Morgan,' she said quickly, before he could say anything, 'when we're married…' She paused. He'd visibly relaxed, a huge rush of air escaping his lungs. Oh, it's not over yet! she thought angrily. 'How do you see our lives panning out?'

'I work from home, you study to be an architecht, we both look after your father and also Jack—now that you're a world expert in nappy-changing. We share the cooking. I burn the meal one night, you the next.' His dark eyes glimmered. 'Then,' he murmured, 'we'll take turns to go wild in bed. My turn first.'

She could bear it no longer. Eyes like green glass, she flicked a scornful glance at him. 'Hmm. You're not too good at self-control, are you?'

Morgan stiffened, sensing that this was no tease. He shot a quick look at the group of women at the far end of the restaurant.

'Meaning?' he asked menacingly.

'I *mean*, that you find it hard to keep your hands off any female in the same house. I thought you'd fallen for my abundant charms. It seems I could have been anyone—though preferably blonde—'

'What did they say, Jodie?' he asked, his voice whisper-soft.

She quivered at the granite clench of his jaw, the coldness of his eyes. 'Does it titillate you to keep your liaisons in the family?' she asked frostily. 'To have both my father's fiancée and his daughter in your bed?'

He gave a quick intake of breath. And only she, with her deeper knowledge of him, could tell how overwhelmingly angry he was. To all appearances he was smiling pleasantly and having a casual conversation with her.

'This is not the place to discuss our affairs—'

'Correction. Your affair.'

His mouth compressed. 'Don't judge me yet,' he said with barely a trace of tremor in his voice. 'I'll drive us home. It's not what it seems, Jodie. Don't be upset.'

'Do I look upset?' she said sweetly, producing a saccharine smile.

'Yes. Your skin is taut across your cheekbones, there's a hectic pulse beating in your throat and your eyes are dead. Let's go,' he said curtly.

Hysteria was building up inside her. She needed an outlet. A release of some kind. In silence she slid into the passenger seat of his Mercedes; in silence she endured the journey. Morgan tried to speak to her but she ignored him, and after a while he gave up.

When they got back she poured brandies for them both in the drawing room and then she stood, back to the fireplace, in an attitude of possession. It was deliberate. He would learn that she wasn't to be played around with.

'So. You had an affair with Teresa. Did you father her baby?' she asked, deciding not to beat about the bush.

He let out a short, sharp profanity.

Something terrible happened inside her. Morgan had gone white, his face drained of all colour by the shock of her words. And she took no pleasure in tormenting him. Misery flooded through her, bringing her to the brink of tears.

'Let's get things straight. One thing at a time. Who is his mother?' she flung.

'I told you. He's Teresa's child,' Morgan replied hoarsely.

'And his father?'

Everything depended on his answer. Her life, her future, Jack's, her father's...

'Why don't you look on his birth certificate?' Morgan threw back his head and downed his brandy in one long gulp. Then he looked at her levelly, almost in challenge. 'Your father's name is on that document. He adores Jack. You know that the very existence of the baby has given him delight, hope, something to live for—'

'In that case,' she said, her eyes hollow with despair, 'you are no longer needed. I intend to look after my dying father. It doesn't matter how awful his last days are. I, and I alone, will be with him, because I'm family. I don't care what you do or where you stay—providing you're not in this house...my father's house, I might remind you. Because I will be here. You can visit—he'd expect that— and we will be perfectly civil to one another for my father's sake. And when...when my father dies, I will bring up my half-brother and you will disappear out of our lives for-ever—because you'll only have visited here on sufferance. And without my father there'll be no need for you to come.'

For several seconds he stared at her, the naked horror in his eyes eating like acid into her bruised heart. He tried to speak and couldn't. She knew then for sure that Jack was Morgan's baby and he was facing his worst nightmare.

Time ticked by. She was rooted to the spot by the despair in his face.

Deny it! she begged. Say it *is* my father's baby, that you made a mistake with Teresa and never loved her—say you love me, me, *me*!

He looked diminished. Robbed of energy and life. His whole body was hunched in an attitude of total anguish.

Because she loved him it tore her apart to see him so hurt. But she knew that he'd destroy her if she weakened. He'd insist that she remained with him: first for her father's sake and then for Jack. And she would spend the rest of her days passionately, hopelessly in love with a shell of a man.

'I love you,' he jerked out. 'You love me! We...I thought we'd have our own children together...'

Déjà vu. It was Chas all over again. One more selfish man who thought he had the world and his bit of fluff all sorted: adoring, obedient and pliable—but a tigress in bed.

'It seems I don't love you after all,' she snapped, her eyes flashing sparks. 'Otherwise I'd fall on your neck and say I understood. But I don't actually care. I think I must have been hungry for sex. Chas kept me well topped up in that area,' she said cruelly, hating herself, hating him and what he was doing to her. 'You were right to advise caution. I jumped into your arms when I was vulnerable—for all kinds of reasons. And now I'm jumping out again. I will look after Jack well. He is my half-brother, isn't he?'

No answer. No denial. Perhaps the women were wrong. Morgan surely couldn't give up his baby. He'd say it was his, plead with her for some kind of trade-off, ask for custody...

She passed a hand over her eyes. It didn't matter who had fathered Jack, in a way. She could never trust Morgan again.

He stood there, just breathing. Barely breathing. 'I'll go.' It was a voiceless, silent agreement shaped by an unyielding mouth beneath tragic eyes.

Aching unbearably inside, Morgan turned, faltered, and crouched down in front of the easy chair where Jack had been propped up against protective cushions. Morgan's fingers touched the small hands and were gripped to a series of coos and gurgles.

He could hear Jodie sobbing. Almost blinded by tears himself, his throat closed with a huge lump of emotion, he tortured himself by gazing at his son, loving him through the pain, marvelling at the perfection of the infinitely loved little face.

Everything he had feared had come tragically true. He was losing his dearly beloved child and... He jammed his teeth together to prevent himself from begging for forgiveness. He must not think. Only act. And close his heart before it broke entirely.

Because he would have to come here to see Sam, to see Jodie, Jack...

Abruptly he stood up. Reached inside his pocket for his diary, wrote down his contact number and flung it on the floor. 'You can reach me there. I'll send someone round to pick up my stuff.'

And he walked out blindly, stumbling into a table on his way and reeling as if he were drunk.

Help me to get through this! he implored the fates. Give me strength! Storming out, on the edge of sanity, he slammed the front door. Viciously screwed the key in the lock till the engine of his car roared into life. Scrubbed at his pathetic red eyes with his handkerchief.

A mistake too far, he thought savagely. No more loving. Not ever. Wheels screeched on the gravel. One backward glance in the mirror. Jodie, standing in the doorway, Jack in her arms.

'Oh, God!' he roared in despair, destroyed by the sight. And he hurtled down the drive like a man possessed, everything he loved torn brutally from his grasp.

CHAPTER TEN

THE silence was frightening. She was alone. Bereft.
Morgan's farewell to his baby had been heartbreaking. She
would never forget it for the rest of her life.

She was now beyond tears. Shattered, she slumped into
a chair, knowing she must rouse herself and get Jack to
bed. Already he was whimpering, as if he'd sensed
Morgan's terrible anguish.

Picking him up, she collected the bottle and the baby bag
and stomped wearily back to the nursery. Jack was yelling.
Upset, her nerves ragged from losing the man she'd loved,
she tried to pacify the baby by mimicking Morgan's soothing walk. It didn't work.

Eventually the bottle was ready. She'd never fed Jack
before, and it wasn't easy holding him in the crook of her
arm while he wriggled and jerked and she tried to take the
cap off the teat. Panicking, she wrenched at it.

Both cap and teat came off, ejecting warm milk all over
her. Half sobbing with frustration, she gave her skirt a hasty
wipe with a muslin square and went down for another bottle.

By the time this one had heated up sufficiently she stank
of sour milk and Jack was screaming his head off. He
wouldn't take the bottle for a while but eventually he did,
gobbling away with awful little jerks and sobs.

Then he stopped feeding, his knees drawing up in agony
as he yelled again.

'Come on, sweetheart,' she said, popping him over her
shoulder. Awkwardly she put the bottle down on the floor

and stood up, pacing the room. Jack stopped crying and she transferred him to the crook of her arm again, ready to feed him. He yelled, so she hoicked him to her shoulder and continued pacing.

It was forty minutes before he burped. Shaking with relief and exhaustion, she sank back into the chair. And kicked over the bottle, the teat spinning into a chair leg and thus becoming dangerously unsterilised.

Jodie felt like screaming. There were no more feeds made up. She'd have to start afresh—and it would be ages before the bottles had cooled.

'I'm sorry, I'm sorry, sweetheart!' she whispered, close to breaking point. 'Oh, hush, please don't cry! I can't bear it if you do!'

'Give him to me.'

She gasped. *'Morgan!'*

He didn't look at her. 'Go and do the bottles. I'll keep him amused.'

She didn't argue. Jack's needs came before hers. She handed the baby over and ran down the stairs, mortified that she'd managed so badly. Morgan appeared, carrying Jack and the baby gym. He obviously didn't trust her, she thought resentfully, waiting for the boiled water to cool.

By a miracle, Jack stopped grizzling and paid attention to the whirring rattle, the musical flower, the mirror and squeaky rabbit. Jodie felt her heart-rate settle down to a mere gallop instead of a thousand beats a minute.

'Did you forget something?' she asked in an unnaturally high voice.

'No.'

'You couldn't bear to leave Jack in my incapable hands,' she muttered bitterly.

'I couldn't bear to leave either of you.'

She whirled, eyes blazing. 'Because I'm your ticket to Jack!'

'No!' he cried, vehement with explosive passion. 'Because I love you. Because I can't live without you. Because I will not let you go without a fight. You are my life. You light my heart. Without you I am nothing.'

'Don't!' she moaned.

'Fill the bottles,' he said gently.

When they were done, she collapsed limply into the big armchair by the Aga. Morgan pulled up a pine chair near her and passed Jack over.

She watched the baby feeding peacefully in her arms and wondered how she could have got into such a state. Because it was important, she thought miserably. She wanted to be good at being a mother.

Morgan watched without comment while she finished the feed, winded and changed Jack. Despite Jack having a dirty nappy, she managed to juggle legs, bottom, wipes, cream and clean nappy with some skill.

Drained, she wordlessly handed him back. But Morgan put the baby on the changing mat beneath the baby gym and, taking Jodie's hand, pushed her back into the chair.

He sat down, his knees inches away. 'I had an affair with Teresa,' he said quietly.

'I don't want to know!' she spat, averting her head.

His hand drew her chin back, forcing her to look at him. 'You'll regret it for the rest of your life if you don't.'

She shrugged. 'Go on if you must,' she said in a hard tone. 'It'll be water off a duck's back.'

'You saw what she was like—'

'Beautiful,' she muttered sullenly.

'Cold and manipulative.'

Jodie's eyes widened. 'What?'

'She fooled everyone. Me included. I fell for the woman

I saw, not the person she was. And soon I disliked her. She was rude to waiters and receptionists and anyone she thought was beneath her. She spent money like water. Made emotional demands on me. I told her we were finished. She decided to spite me and deliberately engineered a meeting with your father, knowing how rich he was—and how highly I esteemed him.'

Morgan leaned forwards, his hands held loosely on his knees. Jodie stared back.

'Your father fell for her,' he went on. 'She knew how to flatter and flirt. I tried to dissuade him and we had our first row ever because he was head-over-heels in love. That very night she moved in with your father—and soon persuaded him to buy a larger and grander house for both of them. I visited less and less—'

'But you saw Teresa alone when you did visit,' she insisted, remembering the story about the daily help finding them together. She held her breath. If Morgan denied that, she'd order him out. It would be the end.

'Once,' he acknowledged. 'I'd done some work in the garden for Sam. I was just coming out of the shower when Teresa walked in virtually naked. I yelled at her to get out.'

'Did anyone see you?' she asked hesitantly.

'I don't think so. Teresa yelled back and ran off, then got into some row with the daily—she went through help like a dose of salts—and the poor woman clearly took exception to Teresa's tantrum and walked out... Just a minute. Jack's dropped off to sleep. Let me settle him upstairs.'

'I'll come,' she said grimly, determined not to let Morgan out of her sight. She waited while he organised the baby alarm and then let herself be led into the master suite. She perched on the edge of a chaise longue. Morgan sat on the floor in front of her.

'It is the truth, Jodie,' he said quietly. 'You either believe me or you don't. I can't prove it. All I ask is for you to consider the kind of man I am, and perhaps your father's opinion of me over the years. And then to weigh that up against Teresa's track record and the kind of friends she went around with. Did you like those women?'

She shuddered. 'No—but I—I daren't risk trusting you!' she whispered.

'No. I see that. Let me finish. You know Teresa was upset when Sam didn't honour his pledge to marry her as soon as possible—particularly as she was pregnant. Sam was over the moon, of course. But when he kept stalling about the wedding she became more than upset—that's when she got herself into a raging fury. After a blazing row she ran out of the house screaming abuse.'

'And she was killed,' Jodie said.

Morgan nodded. He passed a hand over his face. 'It was awful,' he said huskily. 'She'd driven into a tree. Sam went berserk. He blamed himself. I couldn't bear to see him so distraught.'

'And how did you feel about Teresa's death?' she asked shakily.

'I don't know. Angry, sad, annoyed, exasperated—'

'Upset?'

He gave a mirthless laugh. 'Not for her. Not in the way you mean. When I saw her, ruined, dying, my heart bled for her. I would have felt the same for anyone in that position—and I had been close to her, whatever I thought of her morals and values. She told me then that Sam wasn't Jack's father. I realised then why she'd been so utterly appalled when I dumped her—and why she'd found a substitute quickly. In a moment of compassion, because she was near hysterical and about to undergo a Caesarean which would almost certainly end in her death, I agreed that I would never tell a living soul her secret.'

'You are Jack's father,' Jodie choked.

His eyes flickered. 'I can't answer that. I stick by my promise. I can tell you that she was close to term, something she hadn't told Sam, who believed the baby was premature. Do the maths and draw your own conclusions. Teresa and I were lovers, Jodie. But only before your father appeared on the scene. From then on I left her strictly alone. I respected Sam. I wouldn't have poached on his own territory, even if I had loved her.'

'You were devastated by her death,' she said dully.

'By the consequences of her death,' Morgan replied. 'Sam was dangerously ill. I had a baby on my hands. I had to arrange Teresa's funeral and tell lies about how much she would be missed, knowing that my—that Jack,' he corrected, 'would be registered and recognised as Sam's child. And because Sam was so ill—and had been ecstatic about the prospect of a baby, which was all he had left of Teresa—I knew I couldn't break his heart by claiming Jack as my own.' His hand touched hers tentatively. 'What would you have done, Jodie, in my place? How do you choose? The painful, terrible truth, or the silent, protective deceit? I've paced the floor hour after hour, willing some solution to present itself, but to no avail. I kept silent for Sam's sake. It's as simple as that.'

'Sam's or Teresa's?' she asked bitterly.

'It wouldn't have done your father any good to know that she'd deceived him over who'd fathered her baby,' he replied heavily. 'So it was all for his sake, because I knew he was dying.'

'You would have adopted Jack?'

'I would.'

'Then I came along and flung all your plans into disarray!'

He smiled at that. 'You flung me into disarray,' he said drily.

'Until you hit on the perfect solution. If you married me, you'd never lose Jack!' she wailed.

His shock was too profound to be anything other than genuine. 'How can you say that?' he yelled, jumping up angrily. 'I proposed to you because I love you! I'm crazy about you. I think of you all the time. You must know that!'

Her heart thudded. Yes, she did. He loved her. Had never really loved Teresa. She couldn't even imagine them together now. Everything he'd said with such fervour had tallied with the actions of a man who'd placed himself in an impossible position: protecting her father, protecting Teresa for her father's sake and trying to do the best for Jack. She was filled with compassion. He'd never thought of himself. A truly selfless man.

She sighed.

'Jodie,' he said roughly, 'I can see how it looks. Marrying you *is* the solution to all my problems. A wonderful, amazing twist of fate that I hardly believed could have come my way! But if you think I'd ever marry someone for convenience then you don't know me!' he stormed. 'Marriage is too special, too precious to play around with! I wouldn't have anyone as Jack's stepmother just to provide a female body in the house, no matter how sexy or inventive she might be in bed, even though her hair smells of warm silk and her body drives me mad! Even if she makes me feel warm and contented and I feel as if I've found a life-long friend... What are you doing, Jodie?' he scowled savagely.

'Tucking a bit of hair behind your ear,' she answered demurely. 'You're rambling, Morgan. Betraying your feelings. So now I'm going to kiss you... And now I'm going to whisper something in your ear.'

'*Jodie…?*'

'I love you,' she breathed, nibbling his lobe. 'Now all you have to do is to persuade me very, very thoroughly that you love me too.'

'Uh.' He jerked as she undid a button on his shirt and slid her hand inside to rest on his chest. 'I could shower you with diamonds…' He let out a gasp when she shook her head and slowly undid his belt. 'Buy you a yacht?' he asked shakily. She smiled, flinging the belt to the ground and concentrating on shrugging off his shirt. 'Yellow thigh boots. Ferrets. Steak and kidney pie with rich gravy…'

'Idiot,' she said fondly. And, grabbing his tie, she led him to the bed. 'Just love me,' she husked, opening her arms to welcome him.

Life was perfect, Morgan mused dreamily the next morning, waking with Jodie nestling against him. Soon she would meet up with her father and they'd be living here together, as a family.

But then he frowned, as guilt and regret spoiled the paradise he'd conjured up. He would still be deceiving Sam—and now Jodie would be forced to lie to her own father too, every time they referred to Jack as Sam's baby. Their motives were honourable, but the very act of lying to Sam was souring the idyll, and suddenly Morgan's happiness had a bitter edge to it.

And yet he could do nothing, because of his solemn promise to a dying woman.

It was with mixed feelings that he took Jack along as usual on his visit to Sam that day, and he winced when Sam asked fondly, 'And how's my little boy?'

Morgan handed over Jack and struggled to divert his pain and guilt, gently, slowly telling Sam of the circumstances surrounding Jodie's arrival while the older man listened intently.

Once or twice Morgan's attention wavered, his thoughts and his mind occupied with the conspiracy he and Jodie would be indulging in where Jack's parentage was concerned. With a wry smile, Sam brought Morgan back on track until the story had been completed.

'So Teresa caused this hiatus,' Sam observed after a pause.

'She only destroyed Jodie's letters because she was insecure,' Morgan explained generously. 'She couldn't bear the thought of not marrying you.' He put his hand on Sam's bony shoulder. 'We can't turn back the past. We have all made mistakes. But Jodie desperately wants to see you. She's very special, Sam.'

The older man remained silent for a time and Morgan sat quietly, waiting for his decision. He'd already sung Jodie's praises and it had touched and heartened him to see the tears of pride forming in Sam's eyes.

Jack stirred and cooed happily, flailing his tiny arms about. Morgan gazed at the baby lovingly.

'I'd like to see her too,' Sam said, his voice choked. He took a deep breath and held out Jack, an odd expression of determination on his face. 'Take your son and tell her to come. Bring her to me in the morning.'

'That's wonderful!' Grinning inanely, Morgan leapt to his feet and took Jack eagerly, hugging him close in delight. 'She'll be thrilled! You'll love her!' There was an unusually wistful smile on Sam's face and Morgan hesitated, puzzled by it. 'What's going on? What did I say?' he demanded.

'It's what you didn't say,' Sam said shakily. He drew himself more upright against the pillows. 'You didn't express surprise when I referred to Jack as your son.'

Morgan stared, appalled, incapable of saying anything.

'I imagine,' continued Sam very quietly, 'that this might be one of the mistakes you were talking about.'

The world seemed to lurch, falter, and right itself again. 'Sam!' Morgan floundered hoarsely, knowing he should bluster this out, searching for words which wouldn't come. 'I—I—!'

'Don't deny it!' Sam said fiercely. 'I deserve better than that!'

'Oh, God!' Morgan whispered in horror. 'What have I done?'

With a groan of despair, he sank into the chair again, his head bowed, his free hand covering his face. He'd failed. What would this do to Sam? Jack meant everything to him. And now in a stupid moment of inattention he'd destroyed Sam's happiness, his hopes and his joy of fatherhood.

He knew how deeply a father felt. If Jack were to be torn from *him* he'd be distraught... Fearing for Sam's well-being, Morgan raised his heavy head to stare at the older man with the bleak, tortured eyes of a man in purgatory.

This would be the end to his imagined scenario of a happy family. Sam would never speak to him again and would die with loathing in his heart... Morgan winced from the slice of pain which stabbed him through and through. He loved his substitute father more than he'd ever known.

And now Sam was leaning forwards, tears in his pale eyes... Morgan prepared himself for the inevitable rejection, agonising over the possible consequences for Jodie and her hoped-for reunion. He hung his head again, a broken man, haunted by the thought that he'd probably ensured that Jodie would never meet her father.

And Sam would be left alone, dying by inches, without the care of the people who loved him.

'I can't bear it!' he croaked.

A hand unpicked his fingers, which were digging into his face in brutal punishment. Sam's face loomed close and Morgan jerked his head away, too ashamed to meet the older man's accusing eyes.

'This pains you,' Sam said in a surprisingly gentle voice.

He nodded, the self-castigation unendurable. 'How did you know about Jack?' he managed to rasp in a voice he didn't recognise as his own.

'Observation. I'm an architect. I see things clearly. You look at Jack with a special tenderness and protection. You're besotted with him. When my brain was less fuddled by drugs I realised why that might be so. Morgan!' Sam said unhappily. 'Talk to me! Don't beat yourself up! *Tell me!* Why have you deceived me?'

Wretchedly he dragged together the tattered remnants of his self-control, bracing himself for the ordeal of confirming Sam's suspicions.

'I didn't know until I saw Teresa after her accident. I didn't want to tell you when you were so ill,' he began haltingly. 'I couldn't. Even now...I don't know how—'

'Start at the beginning and continue till you reach the end,' suggested Sam. The startling kindness in the older man's eyes merely served to twist the knife of Morgan's shame. 'Trust me,' Sam added softly. 'I care about you, Morgan, and I can't bear to see you like this. If your motives were right then I will be content. You've given me years of happiness by being my surrogate son. I'm not going to turn away from you now. I believe in you and I think you care for me. Logic tells me there's a rational explanation somewhere.'

The two men stared at one another. Morgan saw compassion in Sam's eyes and felt a little calmer. Falteringly he began to explain the situation. It took a while before the whole story was out. And even then Morgan stuck to the promise he'd made Teresa. He didn't say that Jack was his child. But the truth was glaringly obvious.

'You fool! You utter *fool!*' Sam rebuked huskily.

'I'm sorry! I'd give anything not to have hurt you—'

'So you pussy-footed around, breaking your heart, compromising your own integrity for my protection! I don't blame you. I don't blame Teresa. I understood her very well. I loved her, though I knew her ability to love anyone in return had long been damaged by her past. We're all flawed, Morgan.' Sam sighed. 'What a hell you've been in!'

'I hated deceiving you!' he said vehemently. 'We've always been frank with one another.'

'I would have liked Jack to be my son,' Sam acknowledged. 'But I do have you, and you're very close to my heart. We could say that Jack is my surrogate grandson, couldn't we?'

'Sam...are you sure it's all right? You're not too devastated? Do you feel—?'

'I feel fine. I'm proud of you, of everything you've done to care for me. I owe you a great debt and I haven't lost Jack at all, have I? All I want is your happiness, Morgan. That's the most important thing.'

He embraced Sam, moved by the deep love between them. Both were unable to speak for a moment as emotion claimed them.

Sam swallowed and cleared his throat. 'Just make sure you bring Jodie to me,' he said jerkily.

Still overcome, Morgan rose, a lump in his throat. He felt as if a huge burden had been lifted from his shoulders. His eyes grew bright and his heart raced. 'I'll bring her,' he croaked. Embarrassed, he made a show of adjusting Jack's rucked-up jacket. He found himself grinning with relief and saw that Sam looked more relaxed and happy than he had for a long time. 'Brace yourself,' he advised with a fond laugh. 'She's dazzling—in every way!'

Her hand gripping Morgan's tightly, a silent and pale Jodie walked up the stairs of the nursing home towards her father's room. Pushing the baby buggy beside her, Morgan squeezed her hand in sympathy.

'I want him to like me,' she said nervously.

'He will, darling. He appreciates the use of colour!' Morgan joked with a grin, eyeing her tangerine wool dress and the fuchsia cardigan she was wearing. 'You look wonderful. Here we are. If you look through this small side window you can see him. It'll give you a chance to prepare yourself.'

Unable to speak, she nodded. Through the observation window she saw the painfully thin figure of a tall man, wrapped in a cheerful tartan rug, sitting in a reclining chair. Her father.

Tears sprang to her eyes and Morgan's arm came firmly around her shoulders as her thoughts and emotions churned chaotically.

'I love him already,' she said in a choked voice. 'Particularly after his reaction to you when he realised you were Jack's father. I admire him more than I can say. And I desperately want to make him happy.'

'You will,' Morgan answered. 'Can you see how impatient he is to see you?'

She smiled through her tears. Her father kept glancing towards the door and then at his watch. He pushed back the heavy lick of white hair that had fallen onto his forehead and smoothed it with his hand, then checked the way his open-necked shirt sat, tweaked it, and sat erect.

Her heart went out to him. He was nervous too, anxious that she should like *him*. Deeply touched, she lost her anxiety and headed for the door, giving a discreet tap and hesitantly opening it. She looked up at Morgan uncertainly. He returned her glance with reassuring tenderness, put his hand in the middle of her back and pushed her forward.

'Jodie!' Sam cried, holding open his arms.

In a delirium of delight, she gave a low cry, then ran to her father and gently kissed his wan cheeks. She felt his bony arms around her, heard the breath catch in his throat as he spoke her name again, and buried her face in his neck, too overcome to talk.

'Let me look at you, sweetheart,' he whispered.

Sniffing, she moved back and sank to her knees beside him, scrubbing at her eyes with her handkerchief. 'I can't t-tell you how I feel about seeing you...!' Her voice gave out and Morgan passed her a handkerchief, touching her arm solicitously.

'From what Morgan's told me, I'm sure you will, when you get your second wind,' he teased with a smile.

Jodie laughed, and shot Morgan an amused glance.

'Morgan!' Affectionately Sam held out his hand.

'You're looking well,' Morgan said warmly, clasping it in his.

'I feel wonderful. Hello, Tiddler. Still keeping your father up half the night?' Sam murmured, stroking the baby's sleepy face. He looked up at Morgan with brimming eyes. 'Thank you,' he said passionately, 'thank you for my daughter. For everything.' Earnestly he turned to Jodie. 'This man is like gold. He's the best.'

'I know.' She smiled happily and looked up at Morgan again, her gaze lingering lovingly because he looked as if he might do cartwheels at any moment.

'I thought you might. So when are you two getting hitched?' her father asked with studied casualness.

They both gasped. Morgan began to laugh as Jodie's mouth dropped open. 'How...? Who...?'

'Dozy old man I might be,' he said drily, 'but it doesn't take a psychic to recognise an engagement ring and mutual adoration. Do you two know you hardly take your eyes off each other?'

'No!' Giggling, she kissed him. And, delighted by his chuckle, kissed him again.

'I adore her, Sam,' Morgan said, his hand caressing Jodie's head.

'Of course you do. She's eminently adorable. Takes after me, doesn't she?' her father countered.

'Egocentric, arrogant old man!' muttered Morgan, the twitch of his mouth betraying his amusement.

'Arrogant enough to assume I'll be giving the bride away and not too old that I can't stuff myself into Father of the Bride gear,' he muttered, pretending to grumble. 'And, before you suggest it, I refuse to go down the aisle in a wheelchair.'

Jodie glanced at Morgan in alarm, but he didn't look concerned. 'Then you'd better get off your backside soon and get walking again, you old faker,' he drawled.

Her father laughed. It started as a thin and reedy sound, but gradually became deeper, and she realised the value of healing laughter as the colour came into the sunken cheeks and the thin, pinched mouth filled out.

'Shall we send the wretch away, Father?' she suggested impishly.

'My dearest girl,' he said with a feigned sigh, 'without Morgan and his ridiculous mixture of gentle coaxing and flagrant bullying I wouldn't be alive today. So we'll let him stay and he can continue to gaze at you soppily while you tell me about yourself. To pass the time he can work out a fitness plan for me.'

'I have the very thing,' Morgan said airily. 'Based on a Marine assault course—'

He ducked to avoid the grapes that Sam was lobbing his way and his heart lurched to see the helpless laughter in Sam and Jodie's faces as they exchanged glances.

Sam was on the mend. He knew it would be a brief respite, and that the future was brief, but it would be happy. He and Jodie would see to that. Even now she was plumping up his cushion and deliberately calming down the conversation, talking quietly about her childhood.

Morgan drew up a chair and watched them both in relief. The three people he loved most in this world were in this room and they were happy. That was all he wanted. His hand stole into Jodie's. Their eyes met.

She saw the glisten of tears there and knew she was filling up too. Her father's hand tightened in hers and she heard a sniff from his direction.

'I'm so-o-o ha-appy!' she jerked hopelessly.

The two men laughed fondly, and as they swept her into their embrace she felt a deep sense of serenity. There were three men in her life. And she had more love than she could ever have imagined. She kissed them all: her father, Morgan, Jack. And blissfully settled down to catch up on the past, and to plan the future.

EPILOGUE

TO JODIE'S profound pleasure, her father lived for nearly three years, his mind wandering only a little towards the end. The doctors had expressed amazement, but Jodie and Morgan knew that it was happiness and the sound of laughter in the house that had kept him alive for longer than expected.

'I still can't believe that he didn't suffer,' she said soberly, when they were reminiscing about him, some six months after his death.

Morgan held her close. 'Nor I, my darling. He loved every day, was grateful for each hour that he was alive.'

'I'm so proud of him. He was a wonderful, adorable man.'

'He was proud of you and your ambition to be an architect.'

'Dadad!' came an imperious little voice.

Morgan's face softened and he picked up his small son, swinging him easily into his arms. 'Come on, sweetheart,' he said softly. 'Shall we go and listen to Mummy reading to Jack?'

Little Tom nodded enthusiastically. 'Baby come,' he said, pointing to Jodie's faintly swelling stomach.

'Baby come,' Morgan repeated tenderly. 'Baby can listen too.'

Jodie took Morgan's hand. Her father's death had left a huge hole in her life. But she had Morgan, and her studies, and their work with the homeless, and she had her beloved babies.

'Coming, Jack! Ready or not!' she called in warning.

There was a familiar squeal as the little scamp raced from the bathroom, where he was supposed to have been doing his teeth—but had probably been lining up his ducks in the sink.

Jodie and Morgan laughed and made their way upstairs to sit together on the bed: Jack all scrubbed, his dark, curly hair temporarily smooth and tidy, little Tom tucked up beside his adored half-brother—who kindly pointed to ducks and jam-eating bears—Morgan, his arm around as many of his loved ones as would reach, and Jodie, dressed in stunning scarlet silk palazzos and a low-cut beaded citrus top, her eyes shining, her heart full of love, as she read to the family she'd always longed for.

'Love you, Mummy,' said Jack when the story had ended. 'Love you, Daddy. 'Night, Tom. 'Night, Baby.'

Morgan grinned. 'Gruesome! It's like the Waltons, isn't it?' he whispered.

Jodie glared. 'Penalty,' she decided.

His eyes lit up. 'Oh, good!' he murmured. 'Bed, Tom.' Morgan kissed their son. 'Bed, Mummy,' he drawled, his eyebrows outdoing Groucho Marx.

Jodie giggled, kissed the boys, hugged them and kissed them again. She tucked under Morgan's arm, where she fitted perfectly, and switched off the light.

And on the landing he kissed her. 'I love you,' he husked.

'Down, boy!' she reproved.

At once the elderly Satan obediently slumped at the bottom of the stairs, grumbling.

Morgan laughed with Jodie as they wandered towards their bedroom. 'It is possible to have everything,' he said, pulling her to him on the high four-poster. 'I have you and the children. It's all I could ever want.'

'You'd go without supper? Hot showers? Races up to the Long Man?' she murmured.

'Shut up and kiss me,' he growled.

She smiled a dreamy smile. Their mouths met and she lost herself in his arms, surrendering to the deepest joy any woman could know: the unshakable love of her family and an enduring, overwhelmingly sweet passion for them all...

*Harlequin truly does
make any time special....
This year we are celebrating
weddings in style!*

To help us celebrate, we want you to tell us how wearing the Harlequin wedding gown will make your wedding day special. As the grand prize, Harlequin will offer one lucky bride the chance to **"Walk Down the Aisle" in the Harlequin wedding gown!**

There's more...

For her honeymoon, she and her groom will spend five nights at the **Hyatt Regency Maui.** As part of this five-night honeymoon at the hotel renowned for its romantic attractions, the couple will enjoy a candlelit dinner for two in Swan Court, a sunset sail on the hotel's catamaran, and duet spa treatments.

To enter, please write, in, 250 words or less, how wearing the Harlequin wedding gown will make your wedding day special. The entry will be judged based on its emotionally compelling nature, its originality and creativity, and its sincerity. This contest is open to Canadian and U.S. residents only and to those who are 18 years of age and older. There is no purchase necessary to enter. Void where prohibited. See further contest rules attached. Please send your entry to:

Walk Down the Aisle Contest

In Canada	In U.S.A.
P.O. Box 637	P.O. Box 9076
Fort Erie, Ontario	3010 Walden Ave.
L2A 5X3	Buffalo, NY 14269-9076

You can also enter by visiting www.eHarlequin.com
Win the Harlequin wedding gown and the vacation of a lifetime!
The deadline for entries is October 1, 2001.

PHWDACONT1

HARLEQUIN WALK DOWN THE AISLE TO MAUI CONTEST 1197
OFFICIAL RULES
NO PURCHASE NECESSARY TO ENTER

1. To enter, follow directions published in the offer to which you are responding. Contest begins April 2, 2001, and ends on October 1, 2001. Method of entry may vary. Mailed entries must be postmarked by October 1, 2001, and received by October 8, 2001.

2. Contest entry may be, at times, presented via the Internet, but will be restricted solely to residents of certain geographic areas that are disclosed on the Web site. To enter via the Internet, if permissible, access the Harlequin Web site (www.eHarlequin.com) and follow the directions displayed online. Online entries must be received by 11:59 p.m. E.S.T. on October 1, 2001.

   In lieu of submitting an entry online, enter by mail by hand-printing (or typing) on an 8½" x 11" plain piece of paper, your name, address (including zip code), Contest number/name and in 250 words or fewer, why winning a Harlequin wedding dress would make your wedding day special. Mail via first-class mail to: Harlequin Walk Down the Aisle Contest 1197, (in the U.S.) P.O. Box 9076, 3010 Walden Avenue, Buffalo, NY 14269-9076, (in Canada) P.O. Box 637, Fort Erie, Ontario L2A 5X3, Canada.

   Limit one entry per person, household address and e-mail address. Online and/or mailed entries received from persons residing in geographic areas in which Internet entry is not permissible will be disqualified.

3. Contests will be judged by a panel of members of the Harlequin editorial, marketing and public relations staff based on the following criteria:

   - Originality and Creativity—50%
   - Emotionally Compelling—25%
   - Sincerity—25%

   In the event of a tie, duplicate prizes will be awarded. Decisions of the judges are final.

4. All entries become the property of Torstar Corp. and will not be returned. No responsibility is assumed for lost, late, illegible, incomplete, inaccurate, nondelivered or misdirected mail or misdirected e-mail, for technical, hardware or software failures of any kind, lost or unavailable network connections, or failed, incomplete, garbled or delayed computer transmission or any human error which may occur in the receipt or processing of the entries in this Contest.

5. Contest open only to residents of the U.S. (except Puerto Rico) and Canada, who are 18 years of age or older, and is void wherever prohibited by law; all applicable laws and regulations apply. Any litigation within the Province of Quebec respecting the conduct or organization of a publicity contest may be submitted to the Régie des alcools, des courses et des jeux for a ruling. Any litigation respecting the awarding of a prize may be submitted to the Régie des alcools, des courses et des jeux only for the purpose of helping the parties reach a settlement. Employees and immediate family members of Torstar Corp. and D. L. Blair, Inc., their affiliates, subsidiaries and all other agencies, entities and persons connected with the use, marketing or conduct of this Contest are not eligible to enter. Taxes on prizes are the sole responsibility of winners. Acceptance of any prize offered constitutes permission to use winner's name, photograph or other likeness for the purposes of advertising, trade and promotion on behalf of Torstar Corp., its affiliates and subsidiaries without further compensation to the winner, unless prohibited by law.

6. Winners will be determined no later than November 15, 2001, and will be notified by mail. Winners will be required to sign and return an Affidavit of Eligibility form within 15 days after winner notification. Noncompliance within that time period may result in disqualification and an alternative winner may be selected. Winners of trip must execute a Release of Liability prior to ticketing and must possess required travel documents (e.g. passport, photo ID) where applicable. Trip must be completed by November 2002. No substitution of prize permitted by winner. Torstar Corp. and D. L. Blair, Inc., their parents, affiliates, and subsidiaries are not responsible for errors in printing or electronic presentation of Contest, entries and/or game pieces. In the event of printing or other errors which may result in unintended prize values or duplication of prizes, all affected game pieces or entries shall be null and void. If for any reason the Internet portion of the Contest is not capable of running as planned, including infection by computer virus, bugs, tampering, unauthorized intervention, fraud, technical failures, or any other causes beyond the control of Torstar Corp. which corrupt or affect the administration, secrecy, fairness, integrity or proper conduct of the Contest, Torstar Corp. reserves the right, at its sole discretion, to disqualify any individual who tampers with the entry process and to cancel, terminate, modify or suspend the Contest or the Internet portion thereof. In the event of a dispute regarding an online entry, the entry will be deemed submitted by the authorized holder of the e-mail account submitted at the time of entry. Authorized account holder is defined as the natural person who is assigned to an e-mail address by an Internet access provider, online service provider or other organization that is responsible for arranging e-mail address for the domain associated with the submitted e-mail address. **Purchase or acceptance of a product offer does not improve your chances of winning.**

7. Prizes: (1) Grand Prize—A Harlequin wedding dress (approximate retail value: $3,500) and a 5-night/6-day honeymoon trip to Maui, HI, including round-trip air transportation provided by Maui Visitors Bureau from Los Angeles International Airport (winner is responsible for transportation to and from Los Angeles International Airport) and a Harlequin Romance Package, including hotel accomodations (double occupancy) at the Hyatt Regency Maui Resort and Spa, dinner for (2) two at Swan Court, a sunset sail on Kiele V and a spa treatment for the winner (approximate retail value: $4,000); (5) Five runner-up prizes of a $1000 gift certificate to selected retail outlets to be determined by Sponsor (retail value $1000 ea.). Prizes consist of only those items listed as part of the prize. Limit one prize per person. All prizes are valued in U.S. currency.

8. For a list of winners (available after December 17, 2001) send a self-addressed, stamped envelope to: Harlequin Walk Down the Aisle Contest 1197 Winners, P.O. Box 4200 Blair, NE 68009-4200 or you may access the www.eHarlequin.com Web site through January 15, 2002.

Contest sponsored by Torstar Corp., P.O. Box 9042, Buffalo, NY 14269-9042, U.S.A.

PHWDACONT2